There were still a couple of hours of daylight left after the party, so Jack and I took Snickers for a hike in the town forest. "Remember the time you brought me on a walk here to look for owls?" Jack said.

Snickers stopped on the trail to bark at a squirrel. "With all that noise, we won't see any today," I said, laughing.

We walked deeper into the woods. Snickers gave up on the squirrel and started chasing wind-blown leaves. "I can't get over it," I told Jack. "A dog! I've been begging for one *forever*. How did you get Mom to go along with this?"

"I begged for a month."

I had to laugh at that. "Well, I have to say that it was worth it, as far as I'm concerned," I told him. "What an incredible day. Can you believe that Rose and Stephen are getting *married?*"

"Well, when you find true love . . . ," Jack began.

Don't miss any books in this dramatic new series:

THE YEAR I TURNED Sixteen

Available from ARCHWAY Paperbacks

THE YEAR I TURNED

I TURNED

Sixteen

LAUREL

Diane Schwemm

AN ARCHWAY PAPERBACK
Published by POCKET BOOKS
New York   London   Toronto   Sydney   Tokyo   Singapore

This book is a work of fiction. Names, characters, places, and incidents are either products of the author's imagination or are used fictitiously. Any resemblance to actual events or locales or persons, living or dead, is entirely coincidental.

AN ARCHWAY PAPERBACK *Original*

An Archway Paperback published by
POCKET BOOKS, a division of Simon & Schuster Inc.
1230 Avenue of the Americas, New York, NY 10020

Produced by Seventeenth Street Productions, Inc.,
a division of Daniel Weiss Associates, Inc.

ISBN: 0-671-00442-5

First Archway Paperback printing November 1998

10 9 8 7 6 5 4 3 2 1

AN ARCHWAY PAPERBACK and colophon are registered trademarks of Simon & Schuster Inc.

Printed in the U.S.A.

IL 7+

For my parents

One

"You really don't have to give me a party, Mom," I told my mother, Maggie Walker, the day before my sixteenth birthday. I meant it, too. Birthday parties aren't exactly my favorite things.

"Should I just throw away the cake, then?" she teased.

We were in the kitchen. Mom had just baked a triple-layer lemon cake with raspberry filling, and now she was using a tiny spatula to etch a basket-weave pattern in the white butter cream frosting.

It looked delicious, and I was sure, knowing Mom—she's a caterer—it would taste even better than it looked. "Of course I want the cake!" I said, smiling. I pushed the long, gold-brown hair out of my eyes, then stuck my hands deep into the side pockets of my faded denim overalls. "I just don't like people making a fuss over me."

"It'll just be us," Mom assured me, "and Hal. And I invited Jack. That's okay with you, right?"

"Sure." Hal Leverett is our neighbor. He's divorced, and Mom is a widow, and they've been dating for a couple of years now. As for Jack Harrison, he's been my closest friend since we were ten. Jack and Hal are both like family.

Mom finished frosting the cake. She offered me the beaters from the electric mixer. "Do you want these, Laurel?"

Of course I did. I grinned and leaned back against the counter and licked the frosting off one of the beaters. The kitchen window was open, letting in a warm Indian summer breeze. "Remember how I used to practically beat Lily up to get the beaters after you baked a cake?" I asked Mom.

Mom laughed. "Poor Lily."

"Poor Lily—yeah, right." Lily is my younger sister. She's thirteen now, and I've been waiting for her to outgrow her "brat" stage for the past thirteen years.

The phone rang; I had to put down the beater to answer it. "Hello?"

"Hi. It's me," said my nineteen-year-old sister, Daisy.

A warm feeling settled over me. "Daze! What's up?" My mom smiled at me, and I smiled back as I pointed to the phone excitedly. "It's Daisy," I mouthed, and Mom nodded.

"Just wanted to wish you a happy day before your birthday, Toad."

"Daisy! Haven't I outgrown that ridiculous nickname yet?"

"Have you outgrown your roomful of animals yet?" she shot back.

I laughed. Back when my dad died, we had to

move out of our huge house and into a two-floor apartment on Main Street in Hawk Harbor, the small town on the coast of southern Maine where I've lived all my life. At first the landlord told us no pets. Since then Mr. Wissinger, who also owns the bakery downstairs, has relaxed his policy a little, so I've adopted as many animals as I could squeeze into my bedroom.

"Anyway," she went on, "I'll be home tomorrow afternoon." She's a freshman at Dartmouth. "I have a soccer game in the morning, but if I leave Hanover by noon, I should be in Hawk Harbor around three-thirty."

"How are you getting here?" I asked. "Bus?"

"I'm borrowing Annie's car," Daisy replied. "What a great roommate."

"I can't wait to see you!"

"I'll drive as fast as I can. Don't start the party without me."

"Are you kidding? Of course we won't. Bye, Daze."

Hal walked in as I hung up the phone. He doesn't bother knocking anymore—he and Mom are always running back and forth between each other's places.

At first it was weird, Mom having a boyfriend. Daisy especially freaked out about it, maybe because she was the one who'd been closest to Dad. Now we're all pretty used to it, and Hal's about the nicest man on earth.

He greeted Mom with a kiss on the cheek, then set a paper bag on the counter. "Party decorations," he explained. "Streamers, balloons, hats, noise-makers."

I rolled my eyes. "Noisemakers?"

Hal took a party hat out of the bag and stuck it on his head. He's an accountant, with brown-gray hair and wire-rimmed glasses and he's at least fifty, but when he smiles, he looks like a kid. "Come on, Laurel. Live it up!"

"Why don't we start decorating?" Mom said to Hal as she wiped her hands clean on a dish towel. "We're going out tonight and we won't have time in the morning because I'm catering that bridal shower brunch."

I thought about making one more plea for a low-key celebration but decided not to. It wasn't that I didn't appreciate them going to so much trouble. It's just that I don't like being the center of attention. When I was thirteen, Jack threw a surprise party for me and invited practically everyone in our class. Even though I knew he had the best intentions in the world, I hated every minute of it.

Now I trailed my mother and Hal into the living room. I tried to reach for a roll of crepe paper, but my mother told me to sit down and relax. So I propped my scuffed sneakers up on the equally scuffed coffee table. We have a lot of really old furniture that Mom says is too beat-up to qualify as antique.

Mom draped crepe paper streamers around the room while Hal blew up balloons that said Sweet 16. "It'll be good to have your big sisters home, won't it?" Hal observed.

I nodded. Daisy was coming home for my birthday, and so was Rose—she's twenty-one, the oldest in the family, and a senior at Boston University.

"Is Rose bringing Stephen?" Hal asked, pausing in between balloons to catch his breath.

"She sure is," Mom answered. Rose's boyfriend, Stephen, goes to Harvard. They've been dating forever. They met in Hawk Harbor when they were about my age; they broke up once or twice, but they always got back together. "Those two don't do anything without each other."

"Quiet around here, isn't it," Hal said to Mom, "now that two of your four girls are away at college."

Mom sighed. "I'm still trying to get used to it." She tossed me a smile. "Not that Lily doesn't make enough noise for four girls sometimes!"

"At least we had an extra year with Daisy," I said. I gave a little sigh; I couldn't help it.

Daisy graduated from high school a year ago, but she put off starting college until this fall so she could work full-time and help out the family. Our father died six years back—his fishing boat was lost in a storm at sea—and Mom's gotten a catering business off the ground now, but money is still tight sometimes. We all pitch in however we can.

Mom gazed at me, her expression thoughtful. "You and Daisy got to be good friends this past year, didn't you?"

I nodded. I missed Rose, but she had already been away at college for three years. I was used to seeing her only on holidays. Daisy had just left, and I still wasn't used to the fact that she was gone. I missed her. A lot.

Hal stopped blowing up balloons. He thumped his chest with one hand. "The old man's lungs aren't what they used to be," he said, chuckling. "Think I'll take a break."

"Let's start dinner, then," Mom suggested.

They went back into the kitchen, and I walked upstairs to my room to feed my pets. I was still thinking about Daisy. She and Rose are both amazing people. Rose is a very good singer and actress. Daisy's a star, too. She was captain of three different sports teams in high school, and she's on a scholarship at Dartmouth. Plus she's an A student, plus she's beautiful, plus funny, plus kind, plus plus plus.

My lab partner, Ellen Adams, who's the middle of five kids, has asked if it bugs me having a big sister like Daisy who's such an achiever. It doesn't. I don't feel like I have to follow in her footsteps. I couldn't even if I wanted to!

After Alfalfa, my rabbit, was taken care of, I fed my iguana, my turtles, and my tropical fish. As I was pouring birdseed into Lewis and Clark's bowl— they're parakeets—the door to my room banged open. "Where's my Discman?" Lily demanded.

As I mentioned before, my younger sister is a brat with a capital *B*. Sometimes I can't believe we share the same DNA. "I don't know," I replied, "and did you ever hear of knocking?"

"You borrowed it yesterday and I haven't seen it since," she shot back in an accusing tone, hands on her hips.

I gave her a cold stare. She had on a white ruffled shirt with a black bow tie and vest—Lily's into putting together funky outfits. Today she looked like a waiter, but I didn't say so. She's always antagonizing me, but I try not to pick fights unless she forces me to. "I left it in your room," I told her.

"Then why can't I find it?"

I shrugged. "It's kind of a pigsty in there."

"*My* room's a pigsty?" Lily wrinkled her nose and took a sniff. "It smells like cow manure in here. Or is that your hair, which you probably haven't washed in a month?"

I'd washed my hair that morning, but I decided not to dignify her question with a reply. For about the millionth time, I silently thanked heaven that Lily and I weren't sharing a room anymore, like we had to before Daisy and Rose moved out. "Close the door behind you," I suggested.

Lily didn't just close the door—she slammed it. Turning to the parakeets, I sighed. "Sorry, guys. It's not true about the cow manure. You smell fine."

When everyone was fed, I lifted Alfalfa from his cage. Walking over to my bedroom window, I looked out at the boats in the harbor.

I've got a great view, which makes up for the fact that the room is small. That was the only good thing about Daisy's going off to college: inheriting her bedroom. I can decorate it however I want without having to argue with Lily, whose clothes used to take up our whole closet. There's space for all my animals, and I salvaged an old rocking chair that Mom wanted to give to charity—it's the chair she rocked us in when we were babies.

I sat there now with the bunny on my lap. I *did* like having my own room; still, I'd rather have had Daisy back. It was lonely sometimes. Lily and I were the only sisters left. And we'll never be friends, I thought.

"It's cold," Jack said.

"No, it's not," I replied.

"Feels like a frost." He turned up the collar of his denim jacket.

I took a deep breath of woodsy October air. "I think it's nice. Perfect, in fact."

"My battery's dying." Jack's flashlight flickered and went out. A second later I heard him stumble on a tree root. "Ouch!"

I had to laugh. Moonlit expeditions with Jack are always like this. He moans and groans, pretending I'm dragging him out against his will, but then ends up having as much fun as I do.

Tonight we were hiking up a path not far from his house. When we got to the top, we were in Meredith's Meadow, one of the highest spots in town. Jack spread an old quilt on the dewy grass while I pulled out my binoculars. "There's Jupiter," I said, pointing the binoculars skyward. "Just above the horizon. See?"

Jack took the binoculars and looked through them. "Doesn't it have a bunch of moons?"

"Yeah, but we'd need a telescope to see them."

We lay back on the blanket, the binoculars and an open bag of potato chips between us. Looking up at the sky, we took turns naming the constellations: Perseus and Andromeda, Aries the ram, Cepheus and Cassiopeia.

"Even with the moon almost full, there are still so many stars," Jack said after a minute.

"That's what's good about living in the country instead of the city. No lights from buildings and stuff to dim the stars."

"There are other solar systems besides ours, right? Do you think somewhere out there a couple of kids are lying in a field looking through binoculars at us?"

I laughed. "Maybe."

I sat up and wrapped my arms around my knees. Jack was munching potato chips. Without speaking, he stuck the bag out and I took a handful.

Jack and I have known each other almost forever, since the summer before sixth grade, when he moved to Maine with his parents. He was sort of a prissy little kid back then—his clothes were always spotless and pressed. Meanwhile, I was usually covered with grass stains and mosquito bites. For some reason, though, we hit it off. Maybe because we were both a little lonely. My father had just died and Jack didn't know anyone else in town yet, and since he's an only child he didn't have brothers or sisters to play with.

We're still best buddies even though we've changed over the years. Now I turned to look at him in the moonlight. He has thick, straight brown hair and green eyes. According to the majority of the female population at South Regional High School, he's gotten pretty cute. He's popular, too. Sometimes I think that if we hadn't been friends forever, Jack would never want to hang out with someone like me.

Jack noticed me staring at him. "Your hair's frizzing out."

I lifted a hand. My long hair was going wild— the damp sea air does that to me. "Yeah, I forgot a ponytail holder."

"I bet that's what Meredith looked like," Jack speculated.

Meredith's Meadow is named for a colonial girl who supposedly came up here to look at the ocean and wait for her seafaring lover to return. I laughed. "If I look like Meredith, then no wonder that guy never came back!"

Jack just looked at me.

I gazed back up at the sky.

We sat quietly for a couple more minutes. I was thinking about how maybe I wasn't that different from eighteenth-century Meredith. We both loved this high, wild meadow. Both of us knew how to wait for people we loved to return.

"What's that smell? Flowers or something?" Jack asked.

I breathed in deeply. The meadow had a faded,

autumnal sweetness. I didn't need to turn on my flashlight to identify the plants and grasses that surrounded us. "Meadowsweet and oxeye daisy," I told Jack. "Calico aster, burdock, nodding thistle. And smell the licorice? We must have put our blanket down on the last of the sweet goldenrod."

"Everything's dying, huh?"

"Yeah, but that's when the fields are the prettiest, I think. The bunchgrass is turning red now—we should come back in daylight."

"That would be great."

We packed up our stuff and headed back down the dark trail. At the road we said good-bye. "See you tomorrow at your birthday party," Jack said.

"Don't bring a gift, okay? I don't need anything."

Jack's smile was bright in the moonlight. "Are you kidding? I already got you a present. I know you're going to love it."

"Really?" I was curious in spite of myself. "What is it?"

"Nice try, Walker. Catch you later."

"Bye."

We walked off in opposite directions. All the way home I wondered what Jack was going to give me for my birthday. I've always hated getting presents. Everyone gathers around and stares as you open them—it's so embarrassing. That's the problem with birthday parties in general. But still, even though I don't usually like parties, I had to admit that I was starting to get a little excited about this one.

Two

The next morning was Saturday, so I rode my bike to the Wildlife Rescue Center, where I volunteer. Pedaling through town, I thought how nice Hawk Harbor looks in the fall. Pretty soon a lot of stores and restaurants would close for the winter, but during foliage season we still get tourists.

The shop windows held displays of pumpkins and wheat sheaves, and Indian corn was on all the doors. Flags fluttered in front of the town hall. Everyone was outside enjoying the sunny, mild weather. Mr. Appleby stood in front of his hardware store, talking to Patsy, who runs the local diner. Mrs. King, who owns Cecilia's, a boutique where Rose worked for a long time, was setting up sale racks on the sidewalk. The town veterinarian waved to me as he got out of his pickup truck in front of the animal clinic.

"How's the bunny?" he called.

Alfalfa was taking antibiotics for the snuffles. "Much better," I called back as I sped by. "Thanks, Dr. Grady."

I followed the coast for a mile and then turned inland. The Wildlife Rescue Center is in a renovated barn near Goose Creek. I've been volunteering there for a couple of years, and today, if I could get up my nerve, I wanted to talk to the director about becoming a regular part-time staffer now that I was sixteen.

Inside, I peeked into the office. Griffin, the guy who runs the center, was reading e-mail and drinking *chai* tea. Just ask him, I told myself. But another inner voice was louder. *Why would he want to pay you? It's not like you do anything someone else couldn't do just as well or better. You're lucky they let you stick around at all.*

I started to walk away from him, but Griffin had spotted me. "Greetings," he called.

I doubled back to the office doorway. "Hi."

Griffin was a hippie when he was young, and he still wears beat-up sandals, old blue jeans embroidered with peace signs, and a ponytail. He waved at the battered lawn chair across from his desk that's reserved for guests. The WRC is nonprofit, and the facilities aren't fancy. "Have a seat, Laurel," he invited sociably. "What's new?"

I sat down, folding my hands on my knees. "Not much. Today's my birthday."

"Cheers." He lifted his mug of tea in a salute. "Sixteen, right?" I nodded. "Gonna look for a real job?" he asked.

This was my opening, but, predictably, my mouth went dry and I couldn't get my tongue to work properly. "Um . . . uh . . . yeah," I stammered. "But, you know, well . . ."

"Do you like working here?" Griffin asked.

I managed to spit out the words. "Yes, very much. I was actually wondering if I might . . . you might . . . we might . . ."

"Do you want a job? You're hired," Griffin cut in. "I can only pay you minimum wage, but fill out a couple of forms and it'll be official. Okay?"

I could feel my mouth drop open a little. That was so easy! I thought. "Thanks, Griff." I know my eyes were glowing. "I promise I'll work really hard."

"I know you will. I wouldn't want you on the staff if I thought you were a slouch," he said.

I stood up shakily and practically floated back to the wild animal infirmary. My first real job! I thought. I practiced telling people about it in my head: "I work at the Wildlife Rescue Center. Yeah, it's really good experience. I'm going to be a wildlife biologist or else a vet like Dr. Grady."

Carlos Alvarez was mopping the floor of the operating room. Carlos is nineteen—he's studying environmental science at the state university. He worked at the WRC full-time over the summer, and since the school year started, he comes in every Saturday.

He and I don't usually talk a whole lot. I'm shy around everybody, but especially around guys (except Jack) and *especially* older guys (except Stephen). Plus Carlos is really cute, which makes me even more self-conscious. Today, though, I was bursting with my news. "Guess what?" I said. "I'm not a volunteer anymore—Griffin just hired me!"

Carlos has dark eyes and short black hair. He's quiet, but when he smiles, which he did now, it lights up the room. "Excellent!"

"It's the best birthday present I can imagine," I confided.

"It's your birthday?"

Suddenly I felt a little stupid. I didn't want him to think all I did was talk about myself. "It's no big deal," I said quickly.

"Sure it is. How are you going to celebrate?"

"My big sisters are visiting. I'm psyched about that."

"Sisters, huh?" He smiled again. "There are more like you at home?"

"They're not like me at all," I assured him. "They're beautiful and smart and popular."

"Well, I bet they don't know the difference between a duck and a grebe," Carlos said. "And could they pull porcupine quills from a bear cub's nose?"

I laughed. "They wouldn't want to!"

Carlos leaned on the handle of the mop. "What I'm trying to say is, I'm glad Griff hired you. I was going to tell him he should. You're really good with the animals."

I blushed. "Thanks," I said shyly. I hadn't realized he thought I was doing such a good job. In fact, I hadn't realized that Carlos had noticed me at all.

"I'm still your boss, though," he reminded me.

"Okay, boss. What do you want me to do today?"

He reeled off a list of chores: feeding animals,

cleaning cages, giving medicine. I got busy, but I didn't stop smiling. What a great day—I got hired for my dream job and Carlos said he thought I was a good worker! I couldn't wait to tell my family, especially Daisy. She and I always talk about how maybe someday she'll be a doctor and I'll be a vet and we'll both move back to Hawk Harbor. I'll take care of the sick animals, and she'll take care of the sick people—we'll have the whole town covered. My first job, I thought. My first job!

"Happy birthday, Laurel!" seven voices shouted loudly as Mom carried the cake, sparkling with sixteen candles, to the table.

We'd just stuffed ourselves with Mexican food because it's my favorite. Now everyone waited for me to blow out the candles so we could start in on the cake. "Time's a wastin'," Lily pointed out. She'd already told me ten times that we needed to hurry up because she had a date to go to the mall with her friends.

"Okay, here goes."

I blew out the candles with one breath. Daisy clapped and Jack whistled. "What did you wish for?" asked Rose's boyfriend, Stephen Mathias.

I put my hand over my mouth. "I forgot to make a wish!"

"Too bad," Rose said. "Sixteenth birthday wishes come only once in a lifetime."

"Did *yours* come true?" Lily asked her.

Rose thought back for a moment and then

grinned. "No, thank goodness. I wished I'd marry Parker Kemp!"

We all laughed, including Stephen. Parker was the rich, snobby boy Rose had dated before she met Stephen. "You can still make a wish, Toad," Daisy decided. "There must be a statute of limitations. If you make it within three and a half minutes of blowing out the candles, it's still valid."

I thought about it, then shook my head. "I have everything I want already." I smiled at Daisy. "Who needs wishes?"

I cut the cake and passed out slices. As everyone prepared to dig in, Rose said, "This seems like a good moment. Are you all listening?"

"What's up, Rose?" Jack asked.

Rose glanced at Stephen. Then she looked at me, a big smile on her face. Rose is incredibly pretty—she has long blond hair and big blue eyes and a perfect smile—but right then she looked even more beautiful than usual. Her eyes were sparkling, and her cheeks were pink. "Stephen and I have decided"—she paused for dramatic effect—"that after we graduate next spring . . . we're going to get married!"

Rose's announcement was met with shouts of joy. A couple of chairs toppled over as we all jumped up to hug her and Stephen. "This is wonderful," Mom said, embracing Rose. She had tears in her eyes.

Jack high-fived Stephen. "Nice going, man."

Rose turned to me. "I'm sorry to do this at your

birthday party, Laurel, but Stephen and I are leaving tomorrow, and everyone is here tonight, and we just couldn't wait to—"

"Please!" I interrupted, laughing. "You're apologizing for the best news I could have possibly hoped for? I'm counting this as one of my birthday presents."

Rose grinned and I grinned back. I don't think I'd ever seen her look so happy.

"A wedding. Great!" Lily clapped. "Can I wear my purple flapper dress and a feather boa?"

Rose laughed. "You're going to be a bridesmaid, silly. I'll pick out special dresses for you and Daisy and Laurel to wear. You will, won't you?" Rose turned to me and Daisy. "Be my bridesmaids? And of course I want you to be my maid of honor, Daze."

A bridesmaid? I thought. That means walking down the aisle in front of a whole church full of people, right? Before I could start worrying about it, though, Daisy said, "Of course we will." She gave Rose a big hug. "I can't think of anything more fun."

After the birthday cake we went into the living room, still talking about Rose and Stephen's plans. "I'm applying to law schools," Stephen said. "Harvard's my first choice, so keep your fingers crossed."

"There are more acting and music opportunities in New York, but we'll probably stay in Boston," Rose added. "There are some good theater companies there. I'm sure I'll find work—I'll get an agent."

"It sounds so exciting and grown-up," Lily commented with a sigh of envy.

Rose grinned. "Doesn't it? I feel like I'm talking about someone else's life—like how can this be happening to me? I'm still in college! Stephen and I *did* talk about putting off the wedding for a year, but . . ."

Stephen put his arm around her and pulled her close. "We can't live without each other. So why wait?"

"You know, the wedding will be great and all, but it's months and months from now," Daisy broke in, carrying a stack of gift-wrapped packages over to my chair. "Meanwhile it's still Toad's birthday."

I flushed pink, but I settled down to open the presents. Rose and Stephen gave me a book of wildlife photographs. In a surprisingly thoughtful gesture, Lily had decorated a spiral notebook to make a bird-watching journal. There was a hand-knit sweater and a sweet card with a seashell on it from Gram and Grandpa—they live in Florida.

The box from Mom was small. "I think I know what this is," I said, smiling at her.

She smiled back at me. "That's the problem with being the third sister."

When Rose and Daisy turned sixteen, Mom gave them each a charm from our great-grandmother's charm bracelet. The gold rosebud went to Rose, naturally—Daisy's was a seashell.

I opened the little box. Inside, suspended from a delicate gold necklace, was a charm shaped like a tiny maple leaf. "It's beautiful," I murmured.

"I thought it was just right for you," Mom said. "It will look natural even with overalls."

Daisy helped me put on the necklace. "I love it, Mom," I said.

Mom kissed my cheek. "I'm glad, sweetheart."

"Thanks, everybody," I said. "You're all so thoughtful."

"Hey, there's one more." Jack jumped to his feet. "I left it in Hal's apartment. Be right back."

Hal and Jack disappeared. I remembered what Jack had said the night before, about having gotten me a special present. "What do you think it is?" I asked.

Mom and my sisters pretended they had no idea, but I got the definite impression they knew something I didn't—they were trying not to smile.

Hal came back in, carrying a grocery bag. "This stuff is from me," he explained. "Accessories."

"Accessories? What for?" Then I saw Jack. He walked into the room, holding one end of a bright red leash . . . on the other end of which was a roly-poly brown puppy with a big bow around its neck.

"Oh," I gasped. "Is that for *me?*"

"Only if you like her," Jack said. The puppy jumped up on my lap as if she knew she was mine. "I can take her back to the pound if—"

"Of course I like her," I interrupted, laughing as the puppy slobbered all over my face. "Don't you dare take her back to the pound!"

"What are you going to name her?" Daisy asked me.

I held the puppy up, looking into her chocolate brown eyes. "What breed is she?"

"Part poodle, part collie, part retriever," Jack said. "A little of everything."

"Name her after Henry," Stephen suggested, referring to a pet mouse I had a long time ago. Henry was famous for running across the dinner table the first time Rose invited Stephen over for dinner to meet the family.

"She's a girl, though," I pointed out.

"Henrietta," Rose said.

I kissed the puppy's nose. "Are you a Henrietta? Nah."

"She's the color of a chocolate bar," Daisy pointed out. "Maybe you should give her a name that has to do with candy."

I smiled. "She's sweet, too. Well, then, how about Snickers?" The puppy licked my face again. "She likes it!"

Hal dumped out the contents of the grocery bag. There were food and water bowls, a brush, a bag of puppy kibble, and some dog toys. Right away Snickers started chewing on a rubber bone.

"Isn't she smart?" I asked proudly.

"A genius," Jack agreed.

"Like Stephen," Daisy put in. "With these new additions we're going to be the smartest family in Hawk Harbor!"

Everyone laughed and I looked over at Rose, who gave Stephen an impulsive embrace. Daisy leaned in and turned it into a group hug. I gazed at

my older sisters—they both looked so beautiful
and happy, they were practically glowing. My heart
was filled with a sudden ache. I wished they didn't
live so far away. And now Rose was going to be in
Boston for another few years. I guess I should be
grateful, I thought. It could be farther.

My gaze shifted. Jack was staring at me with a
funny look on his face. I smiled at him as I stroked
the puppy's silky fur. "She's so wonderful," I whispered. "Thanks."

He gave me a grin. "Happy birthday," he whispered back.

There were still a couple of hours of daylight
left after the party, so Jack and I took Snickers for a
hike in the town forest. "Remember the time you
brought me on a walk here to look for owls?" Jack
said.

Snickers stopped on the trail to bark at a squirrel. "With all that noise, we won't see any today," I
said, laughing.

We walked deeper into the woods. Snickers
gave up on the squirrel and started chasing wind-
blown leaves. "I can't get over it," I told Jack. "A
dog! I've been begging for one *forever*. How did
you get Mom to go along with this?"

"I begged for a month."

I had to laugh at that. "Well, I have to say that it
was worth it, as far as I'm concerned," I told him.
"What an incredible day. Can you believe that Rose
and Stephen are getting *married?*"

"Well, when you find true love . . . ," Jack began.

Just then Snickers galloped over with a stick in her mouth. Jack picked her up and plopped her into my arms. "You know, she's not your only present," he said.

"She's not?"

"Check her collar."

I dug my fingers into the thick fluff on the puppy's neck, feeling for her leather collar. There was something silver twined around it. "What . . . ?" I looked at Jack in surprise.

It was a bracelet. "They're dolphins," he said, indicating the links of the delicate chain.

I unclasped the bracelet, then dropped Snickers back onto the path. She promptly took off after another squirrel. "It's so pretty. Why didn't you give it to me before?"

Jack shrugged, his hands in the pockets of his khakis. "I guess I felt funny in front of your family. Like, you know, Stephen might give me a hard time."

"You shouldn't have," I told him.

"Why not?"

"Because . . ." My words trailed off as a blush stole up my neck to my face.

My mind flashed back on a memory of eighth grade. For some reason, Jack had asked me to go steady with him. I'd said no way, of course. One night at a party, playing spin the bottle, though, we ended up kissing. It was totally awkward, so after that we both agreed we weren't meant to be a couple. Jack knows I have absolutely no interest in him and me *ever* getting romantic. In fact, I have no interest in romance *period*. But this bracelet seemed like . . . well . . . a "romantic" kind of gift.

"Um, I was hoping that . . ." Jack studied my beet red face. "You know, that you might . . ."

I turned away from him. "Snickers!" I called, clapping.

"Uh, hoping that you'd like the dolphins," Jack finished. "Don't worry. It doesn't mean I'm secretly in love with you or anything."

"Oh!" I gave a little laugh that I hoped sounded perfectly relaxed. "I'd never think anything like that." The truth was, I was relieved. I'd really hate for anything to jeopardize my friendship with Jack, and if he liked me more than I liked him, it would just be too strange.

I stuck the bracelet in my pocket and grabbed Snickers so I could clip her leash back on. "Don't know about you, but I'm ready for another piece of birthday cake."

"Me too," Jack said.

The next morning Rose and Stephen went out to brunch with Rose's high school friend Roxanne Beale. Rose was planning to ask Rox and two other old friends, Cath Appleby and Sumita Ghosh, to do readings and sing in the wedding. Daisy set out on a long run, and Mom and Lily went to church. I sat on the curb out front of Wissinger's Bakery, my bicycle leaning against the brick building, and waited for Jack. After our hike the night before, we'd made a date to ride out to McCloskey's Farm to pick apples.

At ten-thirty Jack pulled up, but not on his bike. "Wow!" I said when he climbed out of the blue Mustang. "Nice wheels!"

"Dad bought it used," Jack said with a proud grin, "so we have an extra car now that I have my license."

I stood up and walked around the car, wishing my family had enough money to get an extra car. And such a nice one, too! I'm not really into cars, but this one looked like it would be really fun to cruise around in. I looked up at Jack, suddenly excited. "Should we drive to McCloskey's, then? Let me just put my bike back inside."

"Actually . . . I have to cancel."

I felt my smile slide off my face. "What's up?" I asked him.

"Well, Ashley Esposito just called. We're going to Patsy's for waffles."

"Oh?" I folded my arms across my chest, frowning. Ashley Esposito is a cheerleader. She has big hair, and other parts of her anatomy are prominent, too. "So you drop everything for waffles?"

Jack shrugged. "Sorry it's so last minute."

"But . . . ?"

"But I thought you'd understand. I mean, you and I are just friends, right?"

"What does *that* have to do with anything?"

"Look, I'm sorry about canceling plans with

you. I am. But I think I might want to ask Ashley out. Is that a problem?"

Jack waited for me to answer him, a funny, watchful look in his eyes. Usually I can read his mind, but right then I didn't have a clue what he was thinking. *Is* it a problem? I wondered. It was, kind of. I was mad—my feelings were hurt that he was blowing me off. And for Ashley! I have to admit, on some level I felt betrayed. But I didn't want to make a scene. I didn't want him to get the wrong idea and think I was jealous because he had a date with another girl.

I still hadn't spoken, so Jack said, "Laurel, I won't go out with her if you—"

"No, no," I said quickly. "You should go. It's fine. I was psyched for a bike ride, that's all."

Jack looked a little disappointed that I hadn't put up more of a fight. "We could always take a ride later."

"Okay," I agreed. "Well, have fun."

"So long."

He climbed behind the wheel of the Mustang and started the engine. Watching him, I had a feeling of déjà vu. It's like eighth grade, I thought, when he asked Tammy Nickerson to go out with him after I said no. But I hadn't been jealous then, and I wasn't jealous now.

As Jack drove off, though, rolling down his window to give me a good-bye wave, I was surprised at how abandoned I felt. The car made him look so grown-up, and there I stood in my old overalls with my bicycle, as if I were ten years old. I couldn't help wondering whether he was leaving me behind.

"Look, they put up a new sign," Daisy said, pointing.

She and I were walking with Snickers down Lighthouse Road to the beach. Our old house had been painted white with pale purple trim. It was a bed-and-breakfast now: the Lilac Inn.

"Isn't it weird?" I asked, tugging Snickers away from some brambles along the side of the road. "People pay money to stay in our old rooms."

Daisy laughed. "I hope they cleaned them up a little."

"Mom went in there once. She said it was totally redecorated. Remember how saggy the porch used to be? They fixed that and all this other stuff we could never afford to."

"Then it's for the best," Daisy said, but she cast a longing look back at the house, and I knew she missed it as much as I did.

We walked fast, a strong wind pushing along behind us. Clouds raced across the sky. "Why didn't you and Jack go to the orchard this morning?" Daisy asked as we cut across the dunes to the beach.

I told her about Jack's brunch date with Ashley. "I can't believe he'd want to go out with her," I said. "I mean, she's pretty, but she doesn't have the greatest personality."

"You're pretty, too, you know," Daisy said.

I knew she was only trying to make me feel better, so I didn't bother replying.

"Does it bum you out that Jack's interested in someone else?" she asked a minute later.

"No," I said firmly. "Definitely not."

"Hmmm," Daisy murmured thoughtfully.

We didn't stay long at the beach because huge waves were kicking up a cold spray. Back on the road, we cut inland to a tree-lined lane that was more sheltered from the wind. "I miss these walks," Daisy said. She gestured to the maples and oaks. "The trees, the rocky beach . . ."

"Dartmouth's nice, too."

She nodded, her blond ponytail bobbing. "The mountains are beautiful. You'll have to come visit me some weekend, Toad."

"I'd love to," I said.

As we passed under a sugar maple tree a gust of wind shook a shower of orange and red leaves down on our heads. We both laughed. "Remember how we'd rake up huge piles of leaves at the old house and then jump in them?" Daisy asked.

"Yeah. And remember the winter it snowed, like, five feet, and you jumped off the barn roof into a big drift?"

"Mom saw me from the kitchen window and nearly had a heart attack. And then she almost *killed* me," Daisy said.

"I built a snow igloo that time and Lily wrecked it," I recalled.

"Because you put up a sign that said No

Little Sisters Allowed," Daisy reminded me.

"She's still a snoop," I complained. "That's one thing that will never change."

Daisy bent to pick up an acorn. She tossed it, and it bounced off an aluminum mailbox with a ping. "When you're the youngest in a family, people are always doing stuff and going places without you. Lily just wants to be part of things."

"She's not a baby anymore, though," I pointed out. "She has her own life and her own friends."

"Yeah, but you're her sister," Daisy said.

"She doesn't even like me! We have nothing in common."

"Maybe someday you'll find you're not as different as you think," Daisy predicted.

We continued along the road. For a second I had a pang. It was so great to spend time with Daisy again. I could be myself with her. She made me forget I was shy—we could talk about anything. I missed her so much when she was gone.

We were almost back to Main Street. As we'd walked, the sky had darkened and now raindrops started to fall along with the autumn leaves. Laughing, Daisy and I ran the last block home.

A couple of hours later, Daisy had packed up her stuff and was putting on her coat. Rose and Stephen had already left for Boston in Stephen's car. "This was such a short visit," I said sadly as Mom, Lily, Snickers, and I walked Daisy downstairs.

"It'll be Thanksgiving before you know it," Daisy replied, putting her duffel bag down in the entryway so she could give us all hugs. When it was my turn, we hugged for an extra minute. "It was great to be with you on your birthday, Laurel," she said softly. I pressed my cheek against her sweet-smelling hair. "This is going to be your year. I just know it."

Daisy gave me one more squeeze and then we stepped apart. Mom, Lily, and I crowded around the door to watch her sprint out to Annie's little white Toyota. It was dusk and still drizzling. Daisy opened the hatch to toss in the duffel bag and then jumped into the driver's seat. Her blond hair was bright against the rainy darkness. "Bye!" Lily and I called after her.

"Drive safely!" Mom added.

Daisy started the engine and switched on the windshield wipers just as the rain began to fall in earnest. Then she drove off, with us waving until she was out of sight.

Mom, Lily, and I were quiet as we climbed the stairs back up to the apartment. Even Snickers seemed a little subdued.

Just us three again, I thought with a sigh.

I went to bed, but I didn't fall asleep right away. Usually I like rain, but tonight for some reason the steady drumming on the roof sounded bleak and foreboding. No matter how hard I tried, I couldn't doze off. When the telephone rang, I sat up abruptly. Who could be calling so late?

A minute later I snuggled back under my comforter. A wrong number, I thought.

Then the door to my bedroom swung open, banging loudly against the wall. Mom stood there in her long white nightgown, silhouetted by the light from the hall. "What is it, Mom?" I asked.

I couldn't see her expression, but the instant she spoke, I knew something was horribly wrong. "That was the New Hampshire state police," she told me, her voice shrill with fear. "There was an accident."

"Daisy," I gasped.

Three

Dawn on Monday was dark and cold. The rain had ended, but the air was still heavy with moisture. Sitting by the front window, Lily and I heard the foghorn moaning off Rocky Point. It was an eerie sound.

"When do you think they'll get home?" Lily asked. After the phone call Mom had dressed and then gone over to get Hal. The two of them had driven together to the hospital in New Hampshire where Daisy had been taken by ambulance. Unable to go back to sleep, Lily and I had stayed up all night. We were both still in our nightgowns—she was wrapped in a crocheted afghan with just her face peeking out.

"I don't know." I pulled my flannel bathrobe up to my chin. "I'm sure Mom will call if Daisy can't leave the hospital right away and she needs to stay with her."

We continued to stare out the window. "Maybe we should call the hospital and find out what's going on," Lily suggested.

"We don't even know what hospital it is," I reminded her.

"We could call New Hampshire information," Lily said. "Or the state police. Maybe they could—"

Just then the headlights of a car sliced through the fog on Main Street. Hal's new Subaru pulled up to the curb. Lily and I watched Hal help Mom out of the car. Daisy wasn't with them.

"She must still be in the hospital," Lily said, chewing her lip anxiously.

"I hope she didn't break her leg or something," I said. "Remember how awful it was when she tore her ligaments junior year in high school and couldn't play sports?"

"What if it's worse than that, though?" Lily's face was pale. "Like a coma?"

"It isn't," I said softly. "Daisy will be fine."

We went into the front hall. A key rattled in the lock. The door swung open. Instead of coming in, though, Mom paused in the doorway. Hal was behind her, his hand resting protectively on her shoulder.

The moment I saw her face, I knew the news wasn't good. Her eyes were red, and her skin was blotchy. She'd been crying. "Mom?" Lily said, her voice trembling with the question we were both suddenly afraid to ask.

"Girls," Mom began. "Your sister is . . . Daisy is . . ."

Mom covered her face with her hands. Hal put his arms around her.

"No," I whispered. My whole body went cold with dread. *No no no no no no no . . .*

The words tore themselves from Mom's throat in a raw, heartbroken sob. "Daisy is dead."

I'm not sure how long Mom, Lily, and I stood there, hugging one another and crying. At some point Mom collected herself enough to call Rose. While Hal made breakfast, Lily and I managed to get dressed, but then the four of us just sat at the table with plates of eggs and bacon and toast sitting untouched in front of us. No one could eat.

I kept my head down and hoped no one noticed the tears that were falling on my omelet. I took a sip of orange juice but choked on it. I spent the next few minutes taking deep breaths and collecting myself.

Rose and Stephen left Boston the minute they got Mom's call—they reached Hawk Harbor around eleven. When they burst into the apartment and I saw my big sister's grief-stricken face, my own tears began to flow again. "Oh, Mommy," Rose cried, flinging her arms around Mom. They stood that way for a long time, rocking back and forth and sobbing. Stephen looked sort of lost, standing next to her, so I walked over to him and squeezed his hand. He looked down at me gratefully, and I gave him a shaky smile through my tears.

When Rose noticed us standing there, she walked over and hugged me. We were both crying. "What are we going to do without her?" Rose whispered.

"I don't know," I whispered back. And I didn't.

*   *   *

Jack came over at lunchtime and helped my mother make the funeral arrangements. He was very calm, and I was so grateful to have him there that I kept bringing him cups of tea, even though I know he doesn't like tea. I didn't know what else to do. He must have understood why I was doing it, though, because he thanked me every time I brought him one and drank them all.

Somehow we got through the grim, gray day. At dinnertime Daisy's high school coach, Larry Wheeler, came over with his wife—they brought some food. Coach Wheeler and Mom hugged and cried while Mrs. Wheeler preheated the oven for the casserole. I lurked in the background because I didn't know how to act around people who were trying to cheer us up.

"Here's some dressing for the salad," Mrs. Wheeler told Rose, "and a loaf of Italian bread. If you need anything else, you just call us."

Her eyes brimming with tears, Rose hugged Mrs. Wheeler.

The casserole smelled good, but it had the same fate as the bacon and eggs at breakfast. Around the table nobody knew what to say to one another. I racked my brain for a topic of conversation to break the silence but couldn't come up with anything—my social skills aren't that good at the best of times. After a bite or two I pushed my plate away. "Mom, can I be excused?" I asked.

She nodded without speaking.

I went into the living room, but I didn't sit
down. For some reason, being still made me feel
panicky. I paced up and down in front of the fireplace, my arms folded tightly across my chest.

A minute later Rose and Lily joined me. "I
need to do something or I'll go crazy," I told them.

"Throw another log on the fire," Rose suggested.

I picked up a long cast-iron fork and turned the
half-burned logs. The embers flickered as I put a
fresh piece of wood on top of the pile.

"I'm cold," Lily said, huddling close to the hearth.

"The heat's up to seventy." Rose touched
Lily's hand. "You *are* icy, though."

Rose wrapped her arms around Lily, resting her
chin on Lily's head. For a minute the three of us
stared at the fire in silence. I started pacing again.

"It's not fair," I exclaimed suddenly.

"I know," Rose agreed.

"Isn't it enough that Dad died?" I went on.

"Maybe it wasn't Daisy in the car." Lily's voice
was small. "Maybe it's a mistake."

"Mom saw her," Rose said gently.

Suddenly I was overcome by a feeling of help-
less fury. "If that crummy car had had better tires,
Daisy wouldn't have driven off the road," I cried.
"Annie shouldn't have let Daisy borrow it!"

Rose looked at me for a moment. "I want to
blame someone, too," she said finally, "but it was
an accident, Toad. Annie cared for Daisy, too. It's
nobody's fault."

"It still shouldn't have happened." My voice cracked with anguish. "We need her. She's our *sister.*"

Lily's face crumpled; tears slipped from Rose's eyes. Neither of them spoke, and my words seemed to echo in the silent room. *Our sister, our sister, our sister . . .*

Unbidden, a memory popped into my mind. Lily, at age six, was crying over a broken doll. When Daisy figured out what was the matter, she helped Lily bandage up the poor thing. Then she had helped Lily set up an entire doll hospital with a few of Rose's old castoffs. By the end of the day Lily had completely forgotten to be sad over her doll—she was too busy scouring the house for other "patients" who needed help.

Who could stop Lily from crying now? I wondered. My heart ached unbearably.

All at once everything felt wrong to me. It was as if the earth had tipped on its axis or stopped turning. As if the sun hadn't come up and never would again.

"Daisy," I whispered, the name like a prayer on my lips. A prayer that couldn't be answered.

Daisy's funeral was set for Wednesday. Tuesday afternoon, I wandered into the living room and found Rose sitting at the piano. Her hands rested on the keys, but she wasn't playing. "What are you doing?" I asked.

She closed the piano lid with a sigh. "Mom

asked me to choose the hymns for the church service," she explained, "and I remember some of Daisy's favorites, but I can't bring myself to play them."

She got up, and we went over to sit on the couch. "I'm supposed to give a eulogy, too," Rose said. "Do you want to hear what I've written so far?"

I nodded. Lily planned to read at the funeral, too—she was writing a poem—but I'd told Mom I didn't want to. I don't write well, and I turn red and stammer when I have to speak in front of people. I'd have to find another way, a private way, to show my love and respect for Daisy. I knew she would understand.

Rose took a piece of notebook paper from the pocket of her jeans. She unfolded it and cleared her throat. "We're all here because we loved Daisy," she began, "and we loved Daisy because she brought sunshine into our lives. Today let's remember her warmth, her strength, her humor, and her generosity, and hold those memories close."

Rose paused. She closed her eyes for a few seconds, her jaw clenched. She started reading again. "Daisy wasn't only my sister. She was my best friend." Once more Rose had to stop, and this time she lifted the piece of paper, hiding her face. "I can't do it," she whispered.

I put a hand on her arm. "Yes, you can."

Rose shook her head, sniffling. "I thought I'd tell a couple of stories about Daisy, but even the funny ones make me cry."

"No one will care. We'll all be crying, too."

Rose didn't answer. We sat side by side on the couch, our arms around each other and tears on our faces, staring at the mute piano and listening to the silence that seemed to have enveloped the world.

I was up early the morning of the funeral because I hadn't been able to sleep the night before. Every time I'd dozed off, the same terrible dream woke me up. In it, Daisy was leaving for New Hampshire the rainy day after my party. Over and over I watched her climb into Annie's car. Over and over I tried to warn her about the slippery roads, but when I opened my mouth to speak, no words came out. Over and over she drove blithely away, never to come back.

I was putting on a dark plaid dress with a black velvet collar when Lily barged into my room without knocking, as usual. "What do you want?" I asked.

"I don't know what to wear."

My horrible dreams had worn me out and had left me with a feeling of helplessness and an edge of anger. I was about to make a sarcastic comment about how she, of all people, should have just the right outfit for a funeral in her over-stuffed closet, but then I took a closer look at her. In her pink terry cloth robe and teddy bear slippers, Lily looked about five years old, and sad, and scared.

"Come on," I said, softening. "I'll help you."

She shuffled down the hall with me. "It's supposed to be something dark, but it doesn't have to be black," I told her as we inspected her wardrobe. I pulled out a navy blue dress with red piping at the neck and sleeves—pretty much the most conservative thing she owned. "This would work."

"Yeah?" Lily asked.

"Yeah."

"Th-thanks, Laurel," she whispered.

Tears welled in her eyes. Her nose was runny, too. I grabbed a tissue from the box on top of her dresser. "Here," I said.

Lily blew her nose.

"Are you going to be okay?" I asked.

She nodded.

I went back to my own room. It was strangely quiet. Alfalfa stopped eating his hay and looked up at me, his head tilted and both ears flopped over to one side. The parakeets weren't chattering the way they usually did. Even the turtles and fish seemed to be mourning along with me.

I gazed out the window at the heavy, dark clouds. Then, leaning my forehead against the glass, I closed my eyes, a feeling of dread weighing heavily on me. A moment later I heard Rose's voice behind me. "Laurel," she said quietly. "It's time to go."

Our little church was packed. Mom's parents, Gram and Grandpa Sturdevant, had flown up from

Florida the night before. Daisy's college roommates, Annie and Meghan, and her soccer teammates had driven over from Dartmouth. I spotted her high school friends Jamila and Kristin, and Coach Wheeler, and some of her old teachers from South Regional, and her friend Ben Compton, who'd survived a brain tumor. The Schenkels, the Comiskeys, the Applebys, the Beales, and the Mathiases filled a couple of pews, and Jack was sitting right behind me with my friend Ellen Adams.

The organist played some hymns that made my eyes well up. Then Rose read her eulogy. It was very moving, and as she'd predicted, she cried, and as I'd predicted, everyone else in the church did, too.

When it was her turn to speak, Lily looked at me with wide eyes. "I'm scared," she whispered.

"You'll do fine," I whispered back.

Her shoulders rigid, Lily walked slowly to the front of the church. Reverend Beecher gave her an encouraging smile. Clutching a piece of paper in her trembling hands, she turned to face the congregation. She didn't look at the paper, though. She'd memorized her poem.

"Daisy's hands could throw a strike," Lily began in a small but lilting voice. "Or mend a doll, or fix a bike. / They were gentle, they were strong; / Her fingernails were never long— / That would have gotten in the way / Of making dinner, of work, of play. / Her hands were beautiful to me, but she was never vain." She stopped and took a deep breath.

"I'll never hold those hands again. / The lonely wind sighs out her name."

Lily ducked her head, hiding her face behind a curtain of blond hair, and hurried back to the pew. Reverend Beecher resumed his homily. I took Lily's hand and held it tight.

The service concluded with a final hymn: "Amazing Grace." The melody is solemn, but I usually find it uplifting. Still, my heart felt as heavy as a stone inside my chest. I knew that the hardest part of the morning was still to come.

The last notes of the hymn died away. Reverend Beecher gave the benediction. For a minute the church was silent. Then the pallbearers— Hal, Stephen, Grandpa, and Coach Wheeler— carried the coffin outdoors to the cemetery next to the church.

The day had turned cold and drizzly, but Reverend Beecher stood by the new grave with a bare head, his Bible open in his hand. "'The Lord is my shepherd; I shall not want,'" he read. "'He maketh me to lie down in green pastures: he leadeth me beside the still waters.'"

Jack stood next to me, gripping my hand in one of his and holding an umbrella over our heads. I listened to the words of the Twenty-third Psalm, but they didn't comfort me. I felt as if I were standing on a precipice, about to fall. Trying to hold myself onto the earth, I looked at Mom, her face pale against the black of her dress, and Rose clutching Stephen's hand, and Lily standing

between Gram and Grandpa with her little bouquet of daisies.

"'Yea, though I walk through the valley of the
shadow of death, I will fear no evil: for thou art
with me.'"

Lily's face was streaked with tears. So was mine.

"'Surely goodness and mercy shall follow me all
the days of my life: and I will dwell in the house of the
Lord forever.' Amen." Reverend Beecher closed the
book. He looked at Lily, and she stepped forward to
place her flowers on top of the coffin. Then slowly
the coffin was lowered into the grave.

I wanted to run forward and stop them from
putting my sister's body in the ground. I couldn't
stand to think of the weight of all that earth on
her coffin—Daisy hated to be closed in, she liked
the outdoors. . . . A ragged sob caught in my
throat.

Jack squeezed my hand in silent sympathy.
Mom was standing tall, but Rose and Stephen were
both weeping. Meanwhile Lily had not stepped
back. Her body small and hunched and her hair
hanging down, she knelt on the wet grass at the
edge of the grave, as if she could somehow get close
enough to say good-bye.

A few minutes later people began to walk away
across the damp grass to the cemetery gate. Ellen
came over to pat my shoulder awkwardly before
leaving. Jack and I were the last ones left.
"Laurel?" he asked.

"Go on," I said. "I'll be right there."

He offered me the umbrella, but I didn't take it. I didn't care about the rain. Just a few days ago Daisy and I were together, I thought. Remembering our walk to the beach last Sunday and our talk, I realized that I'd never again hear the sound of her voice.

My tears fell with the raindrops onto the fresh dirt of the grave. I'd always depended on Daisy's love and advice. "Who will I talk to now?" I whispered.

There was, of course, no answer.

Four

I went to school on Friday because I knew I would have to sooner or later, anyway. The minute I got there, though, I wished I'd stayed home. Everyone at South Regional had heard about Daisy, and people I didn't even know came up to me to tell me they were sorry. I didn't know what to say in return, so I just mumbled, "Thanks," my face red and my eyes stinging with unshed tears.

Somehow I made it through my morning classes. At lunch I hesitated outside the cafeteria. It was such a public place. Everyone will stare at me, I thought, cringing at the prospect.

I was about to turn away when Ellen appeared at my elbow. She has straight red hair and glasses and freckles, and she wears big sweaters that hang down to her knees. She's only about five feet tall. We're lab partners in physics, and she's about the closest girlfriend I have at South Regional.

Now she smiled tentatively up at me. "Hi. Want to have lunch?"

"I—I'm not that hungry," I said.

"You should eat, though." She gave me a friendly push. "Come on. I'll buy."

47

We got in the lunch line. Ellen slid my tray along for me and picked out a grilled cheese sandwich and an apple. "This okay?" she asked. I nodded wordlessly.

We sat down at a quiet corner table, and Ellen pulled something out of her backpack. "Physics notes from the days you missed," she explained.

I took the sheets of paper, touched by her thoughtfulness. "Thanks, Ellen."

"Just let me know if there's anything else I can do," she said.

The physics notes made me a little sniffly. As I was struggling to keep the tears away I spotted Jack. He'd come into the cafeteria with Ashley and Liz, one of Ashley's cheerleader friends. I could tell they were discussing where to sit. Jack glanced my way, but Ashley deftly steered him to another table.

He put his tray down with hers, then headed over to Ellen and me. Girls at neighboring tables checked him out as he walked past, but he didn't even notice.

I hope he's coming over to tell me a joke, I thought. I needed a laugh. Instead he placed his hands flat on the table and looked down into my eyes. "How're you doing?" he asked, his voice low and full of concern.

Something about the way he said it . . . I don't know, for some reason, his voice made me lose it. "Excuse me," I choked out, pushing back my chair.

I bolted out of the cafeteria, my braid flapping behind me. Jack ran after me. "I need a ride," I told him when we were out in the hall.

Jack didn't ask any questions. He just nodded.

We stopped at the principal's office so I could get excused from my afternoon classes and Jack could get permission to leave school. Then he drove me home.

Inside the apartment it was quiet. All week long there'd been nonstop activity as friends and neighbors dropped by with casseroles and condolences. This morning, though, my grandparents had flown home to Florida and Rose and Stephen had headed back to Boston because Stephen had a meeting with his thesis adviser that he couldn't postpone and Rose had a weekend performance with her a cappella singing group.

I felt dumb for making such a scene at school, so I tried to cover it up with talk. "I wonder where Mom is?" I said as Jack and I went into the kitchen. "Working or doing errands, I guess, but usually she leaves a note, you know?"

Jack bent to open the door to the puppy's crate, which is in the corner next to the refrigerator. Snickers catapulted out and started jumping on him. "She's working this week?"

"Yeah, everybody's trying to throw themselves right back into normal life, I guess. Mom has a couple of parties this weekend. Her assistant, Sarah, offered to take over the catering stuff for a while to give her some time off, but Mom didn't want to.

Do you want something to eat?" I asked, turning to look in the fridge. "You didn't get to have lunch. I could make a sandwich. There's leftover roast chicken."

"No, thanks. I think I'll just head back to school."

I whirled to face him. I don't know why, but suddenly I was terrified of being alone, and I'm sure it showed on my face.

"Unless you want me to stick around," Jack added. "I'll stay if you want, Laurel."

"N-No. That's all right," I stammered, embarrassed that my feelings were so transparent. "You might get in trouble."

"I'm sure I could get an excuse. I'm not worried about it."

"No, I'm okay," I said, even though I wasn't.

We were on opposite sides of the kitchen island. Now Jack walked around to stand next to me. "Laurel," he said softly. "You know I'm always here for you if you need me."

"I—I know," I said, dropping my eyes.

"Like after school or tonight, if you want company. We could go for a hike or see a movie."

I was about to say that I *did* want him to stay with me. Instead, for some mysterious reason, I found myself asking in an accusatory tone, "Don't you and Ashley have a date tonight?"

At this point I wasn't sure what, if anything, was going on between Jack and Ashley. It seemed like a year since the waffles incident last Sunday morning.

They were about to eat lunch together today, though, I recalled.

"We don't really have a date," Jack answered. "I mean, we talked about maybe doing something, but it's not definite."

"Well, don't change your plans on my behalf," I said testily. I don't know why I was feeling so furious. "You don't need to sit around holding my hand."

"All right," Jack said, his expression puzzled.

I turned away so he wouldn't see that once again, I was about to start crying. "I'm really all right," I repeated. I grabbed a loaf of bread and a jar of peanut butter and got busy making a sandwich. "Thanks for the ride." Please say that you know I'm not all right, I thought. Please give me a hug.

"I'll call you tomorrow, okay?"

"Okay."

He waited a minute. I knew he was watching me, but I kept my back stubbornly turned. I certainly wasn't about to beg him to comfort me. "Adios, amiga," he said at last.

Jack's footsteps receded. I heard the front door squeak open and then thump shut. Looking out the kitchen window a few seconds later, I saw him get in his car and drive off. Then, even though peanut butter probably isn't good for puppies, I tore the sandwich into bits and fed it to Snickers.

An hour later I decided that coming home early from school hadn't been the greatest idea. I didn't

have anything to do, and I needed a distraction—
something more stimulating than homework—to
take my mind off Daisy. There's no point in going
outside, I decided. Bright bolts of lightning illumi-
nated the dark sky, and rain pelted the windows. I
knew better than to walk in the woods or on the
beach in weather like that.

I considered my other options. The library?
The mall? I called the WRC, but the machine
picked up. "We're closed right now. If this is an
emergency, contact County Animal Control.
Otherwise call back tomorrow," Griffin's raspy
voice advised.

I wandered aimlessly around the apartment,
Snickers tagging along at my heels. In the family
room I put away some CDs that were lying on
top of the stereo and straightened the couch pil-
lows. Mom had left a grocery bag of canned
goods on the floor outside the pantry, and I
stacked them on the shelves, taking extra time to
separate the vegetables from the fruits and the
soups. Then I had a brainstorm. Laundry! It had
been piling up all week. It was all downstairs already; I just needed to throw it in the washing
machine.

I started a load and sorted the rest of the
dirty clothes into three baskets: lights, darks,
and in-betweens. When that was done, I headed
upstairs to my bedroom. I'll change my sheets, I
thought, and dust the bookshelves and clean
Alfalfa's cage and . . .

I reached my room, but I didn't step through the door. Someone was sitting in my rocking chair.

Mom.

My room used to be Daisy's room before she left for college, and some of Daisy's stuff was still in the closet. Mom had gotten out a box full of sports gear. A softball mitt lay on her lap, and she was clutching one of Daisy's old South Regional High soccer jerseys, the faded cloth held up to her cheek. She was sobbing.

I stood in the doorway, paralyzed. Mom hadn't noticed me yet, and I didn't know what to do. I wanted to comfort her, but I didn't know how.

Just then Snickers bounded into the room, heading straight for the rocking chair. Mom looked up, startled. "Oh, Laurel, I'm sorry." She dabbed at her wet eyes with the shirt. "I didn't know you were—I just—I just—"

The tears started again. Mom bent and picked up Snickers and hugged her as she'd hugged the soccer jersey, grief flowing from her like a river.

I crossed the room and crouched beside the rocking chair. My own loss was unbearable; I could only imagine Mom's. What could I say to make her feel better? Words seemed so inadequate.

I ended up not saying anything. I put my arms around my mother and she rested her head on top of mine while Snickers licked the tears from both of our faces.

On Saturday morning I woke up at dawn and couldn't go back to sleep. After showering and eating breakfast, I stuck a banana and a couple of books in my backpack. Dressed in a turtleneck and overalls with an anorak on top, I headed outside into the misty fall morning.

I still didn't have my driver's license—I was going to take the test in another week—and I had lots of time to kill, so instead of biking I decided to walk the three miles to the WRC.

I set out down Lighthouse Road, then cut across a field to the woods that ran behind the Lilac Inn. I followed a path that hopped the creek and emerged from the trees by the Schenkels' driveway. After another half mile I reached the rocky beach at Kettle Cove.

I sat down on a big, flat boulder and ate my banana, listening to the water rolling and hissing up to the seaweed-covered shore. Past the neck of the cove, fishing boats chugged out to check the lobster pots. My father and his father before him were fishermen, and whenever I'm near the ocean, I think about Dad. This morning, with the newly risen sun shining in my eyes, I tried to picture his face, and for the first time since he died, I couldn't. It had been too long. Will I forget Daisy's face? I wondered, my heart aching at the thought.

Griffin was at his desk doing paperwork when I got to the WRC around eight-thirty. "Didn't think you'd make it this morning," he called out as I hung my backpack on a peg in the hall. He walked out and stood near me, his hands in the pockets of his jeans. "I'm sorry about your sister, Laurel."

"Thanks." I shrugged, trying to look tough. It didn't work. I'm not going to cry, I thought, but it was too late. A tear slid down my cheek.

Under his scruffy exterior, Griffin is a warm and gentle person. He folded his arms around me in a bear hug. "It'll be okay."

"Thanks," I said again, whispering this time.

I cut through the building to the infirmary, where I found Carlos sitting on a table with something round and fuzzy and brown cradled in his arms. "What have you got?" I asked him.

Carlos was trying to stick a baby bottle in the animal's mouth, but it kept wriggling. "Harbor seal," he grunted. "A couple of months old. His mom got killed by a boat propeller." Carlos frowned down at the seal. "He won't take the formula."

We haven't had a seal the whole time I'd worked at the WRC. They don't hang out in the waters of Hawk Harbor anymore. "Want me to do some research and find out what they like to eat?" I offered.

"I already put a call in to the aquarium guy down in the city, but yeah. See what you come up with. Jeez." Carlos's voice cracked. He shook his head. "He's dropped a lot of weight already, you know? I don't want to lose the little guy."

I put out a hand to touch the seal's sleek fur.

"We won't lose him," I declared. "I'll look on the Internet right now."

Carlos met my eyes. For a second he looked young and a little scared—as young and scared as me. Then he managed to smile. "Right. You're right, Laurel. I don't know why I even said that. Just because I haven't cared for a seal before doesn't mean I should panic."

"You'll figure it out."

"*We'll* figure it out."

I turned to head back to the office and Griffin's computer. Carlos's voice stopped me at the door. "I should've said this sooner, Laurel. I'm sorry . . . about Daisy."

It was the same thing people had been saying to me for days, but somehow I knew Carlos really meant it. "Thanks," I told him softly. I hoped he knew I meant it, too.

When I got home, I called Jack from the family room phone. "I was wondering when I'd hear from you," he said. "I called this morning, but you'd already left for work. How are you holding up?"

"Not bad," I lied. "It felt good to be busy, anyway."

"Well, I thought about you all day."

My throat got tight. I decided to get right to the point to minimize the possibility that I'd end up crying. "I just wanted to thank you for bringing me home yesterday," I said. "That was nice of you."

"The least I could do, Walker."

"So, do you want to go canoeing on the river tomorrow? We won't have many more decent days—pretty soon it'll be too cold."

"Actually . . ." He hesitated. "I might be going to the outlets in Kittery with Ashley."

"So you two are really a couple, huh?" I asked, my voice a little shaky.

"I guess."

"You *guess?*"

"It's kind of heading in that direction, yeah. But Laurel, you know, you're—" He stopped and sighed. "Look, I'll call you tomorrow, okay?"

"Don't bother if you're busy." I didn't know why I was acting so sulky, but I couldn't seem to control it.

"I'll call you," Jack repeated.

I hung up the phone, and once again the tears began to fall. How many could a single person shed?

At dinnertime Mom put a meat loaf in the oven for me and Lily and then dashed off to a wedding cake workshop in Portland. When the timer went off, I called upstairs, "Lily, supper."

Five minutes later I'd made a salad, set the table, and poured a couple of glasses of milk, but Lily still hadn't appeared. With a sigh, I stomped upstairs to get her.

Her door was ajar, so I walked in. The room was dim. Lily's desk lamp was on, but she'd draped a towel over the shade. Lily herself was lying facedown on the bed with her face buried in the pillow.

She looked asleep. I won't wake her up, I decided, turning to leave. She can microwave her dinner later. Then I heard a sniffle.

I took a step toward the bed and then hesitated. Maybe Lily wanted to be left alone . . . then again, maybe she didn't. I didn't know what to do. How could I comfort her? I guessed I could say, "I know how you're feeling," but did I? Was our sorrow the same? I don't know how to talk to my own sister, I realized. Not unless we're fighting.

I knelt beside the bed, the same way I'd knelt next to Mom in the rocking chair, and touched Lily's back so lightly, she probably didn't even feel it. At any rate, she gave no sign. I waited a minute, listening to her ragged breathing, and then stood up and tiptoed out of the room.

I didn't go back down to the kitchen and the lukewarm meat loaf. Instead I retreated to my own room, feeling sick to my stomach.

What was wrong with me? I took Lewis from the birdcage, then paused in front of the mirror to study my reflection. My brown hair had come loose from its braid and looked a little wild; my green eyes were big in my pale face. I hugged my parakeet. Why did I know the right thing to do around animals but never around people?

Lewis started pecking at the buckle on my overall strap. I turned away from the mirror to stick him back in the cage, tossing in a handful of seed before I latched the door. Around me, the stillness of the house felt heavy and oppressive, like the air before a storm. The only sounds I heard were Alfalfa munching his hay and my own heart beating in a lost, erratic way.

Five

Fall darkened into early winter, and I alternated between feeling numb and being overwhelmed by uncontrollable emotions. One Monday afternoon there was a special ceremony at the South Regional gym—a plaque was put up in Daisy's memory. Mom and Lily both cried when Coach Wheeler made the dedication, but I sat stiff and dry eyed, as if I were carved of granite. The next day, though, heading to gym class, I spotted Daisy's face in one of the team pictures on the wall outside the locker rooms and I burst into tears.

"I'm not going to be around the next few nights," Mom told me when I got home from school that afternoon.

She was in the kitchen, sifting flour into a gigantic mixing bowl. "What's up?" I asked.

"I'm catering a preconcert event at the Portland Symphony tomorrow," she answered, "and then I'm taking a class at the culinary institute, and I have a cocktail party in Kent on Friday."

"You're so busy! Do you need any help?"

"I think Sarah and I can handle it," Mom replied.

"I'm around, though, you know." I hitched

myself onto a stool at the counter. "I mean, Daisy used to help you with parties when she was about my age. I could at least come along to pass hors d'oeuvres or wash dishes or something. Lily, too."

Mom shook her head. "That's sweet of you, Laurel. I absolutely don't want to burden you two girls, though. No. But thanks, hon."

She patted me on the cheek with a floury hand and then turned back to her work.

Since she didn't need me, I went into the family room, planning to turn on the computer to type up an English paper that was due the next day. Lily was already sitting in front of it, though, as usual. She surfs the net twenty-four hours a day. "I need to use the computer," I told her.

"So do I," she countered, not turning away from the screen.

"You're only supposed to use it for an hour at a time, and only for homework," I reminded Lily. I crossed the room to look over her shoulder. As I suspected, she was in a chat room. "That doesn't look like homework."

Lily hit exit, but not before I saw the last few words she'd typed. "Who's 'lilli'?" I asked her.

She raised one eyebrow at me.

"What's with the lowercase *l?*" I pressed.

"I just felt like a change, okay?" she said defensively.

I took her place in front of the computer.

"What were you and Mom talking about just now?" she asked.

Typical Lily—always putting her nose in everyone's business. "Catering," I said. I couldn't hold back a troubled sigh. "Mom won't let me help her."

"Of course not," Lily said offhandedly. "You'd just screw up."

I frowned. I knew I wasn't as capable as Daisy had been, but it didn't help to hear Lily say so. "Thanks for the moral support," I said dryly.

"Anytime," she shot back on her way out of the room.

I clicked the mouse on my homework folder and propped up my spiral notebook so I could read the notes I'd scribbled for my English paper. At least Lily's back to normal, I thought. For a while there, it had almost looked as if Daisy's death might draw us closer together. That didn't seem too likely anymore.

The following Saturday morning I beat Carlos to the WRC. When he arrived, I was already in the infirmary, feeding the baby seal, whom we'd named Lefty because he liked to wave his left flipper. "He took twelve ounces!" I announced proudly.

"No kidding!" Carlos joined us. "What's the trick?"

"A new bottle," I said. "I bought a bunch of different styles at the drugstore. Lefty likes this one the best."

The seal was still guzzling formula. Carlos laughed. "I'll say."

"Plus I added some pureed anchovies. First I soaked them to get the salt off. I read about that on the net."

"Must be the biggest meal he's had yet," Carlos said.

I nodded.

I started to hand Lefty over to Carlos, but Carlos shook his head. "No, you're doing great. Stick with it."

Carlos went over to the counter to read my notes about the formula. He tapped a pencil on the page. "The expert from the aquarium, Fred, is coming up on Monday," he told me. "He's going to talk to us about how we should handle Lefty so that he'll be ready to be re-released into the wild next summer."

I ran a fingertip along the glossy fur on Lefty's brow. It was hard to believe he'd ever be big enough to fend for himself in the ocean. "Oh."

"Why don't you put together a short presentation for Fred to fill him in on what we've been doing so far? That is, if you don't have anything else going on after school on Monday."

I glanced quickly up at Carlos, momentarily panicked. "No, I can't. I'm really not good at—" Thankfully, I remembered something. "I have a science club meeting on Monday. I shouldn't miss it."

"Are you sure? This would be good experience for you."

"You should give the presentation," I insisted. "You're in charge. You know more than I do."

Carlos leaned back against the counter, his arms folded across his chest, and studied me. "Okay," he said finally. "I don't want to pressure you."

I dropped my eyes and pretended to be busy rearranging Lefty and his bottle.

Did I look like a total wimp? I wondered. Carlos was trying to teach me, to give me more responsibility. "Well, maybe I should give it a try," I started to say. But when I looked up, he was gone. It was just as well. If I tried to give the presentation, I'd only get tongue-tied and humiliate myself in front of Carlos. It was best for me to stay behind the scenes, where I belonged.

Rose and Stephen came home that weekend to help Mr. and Mrs. Mathias look for a place to hold the rehearsal dinner. The wedding date had been set for early June. "I'm stuffed," Rose groaned on Sunday afternoon. "We ate lunch at three different restaurants!"

Stephen had popped over to his parents' house. Rose and I were in the family room, channel surfing. It was raining, for a change.

"I'm glad I caught you before you headed off to the WRC again," Rose said. I'd been running over there a lot lately, even when I wasn't working, to check on Lefty. "I want to talk to you about something." She clicked off the TV.

"What is it?" I asked.

"It's about the wedding," Rose said. "I want you to be my maid of honor, Laurel."

I stared at her in surprise. I have to admit, I had barely thought about the wedding at all lately. It was the furthest thing from my mind. "You mean, because Daisy . . . But why me?"

"You're my next oldest sister," Rose explained. "You're the one I want standing next to me when I take my vows with Stephen."

I knew this was a big honor, but I didn't squeal with delight. The whole idea of taking Daisy's place, of doing her job . . . it didn't appeal to me on a lot of levels. "Wh-what else does a maid of honor do?" I asked nervously.

"Well, usually the maid of honor plans the bridal shower," Rose told me, "and in general helps the bride with stuff, especially on the day of the wedding. You're basically the head bridesmaid. Chairwoman of the board."

Plan a bridal shower? This was getting worse and worse. All of that was the kind of stuff Daisy would have been great at. And it was the kind of stuff that I would totally screw up. "Val's older than me," I pointed out. "She'd probably do a better job."

Valerie is Stephen's twenty-one-year-old sister. She and Rose didn't get along back in high school, but now they're friends. Stephen's younger sister, Elizabeth, who is my age, was going to be a bridesmaid, too.

"It has to be you, Toad," Rose insisted with a

smile. She looked a little sad, though. "Val doesn't even come close to meaning as much to me as you do." I thought about how Rose had said in her eulogy that Daisy was her best friend. It must be really hard for her to ask anyone to stand in for Daisy, I realized. I can't make her ask Val.

"I'll do it," I told her, reaching for her hand.

She smiled and I smiled, too, and that was the end of the conversation. I consoled myself with the thought that the wedding was more than six months off. I didn't have to worry about it . . . yet.

After school on Monday, before the science club meeting started, Ellen and I went to the cafeteria to buy snacks at the vending machine, and we ran into Jack and Ashley. "Hi," Jack said.

Ashley flashed me an insincere smile. I can tell it bugs her that Jack's best friend is a girl. Not that I'm much of a threat.

"Hi," I replied.

I feel uncomfortable around Ashley, so I gave Ellen a let's-get-out-of-here look. Before we could take off, though, Jack said to me, "Science club, right? I'm walking Ash to cheerleading practice, and then I have a wrestling team meeting. We're going the same way."

He was right—unfortunately. The four of us fell into step together. "Science club?" Ashley asked, lifting one blond eyebrow. "How intellectual!"

"We're planning the spring science fair," Ellen told her.

"Think you'll enter this year?" Jack asked me.

I shrugged. I like science—that's why I'm in the club. But I'm not competitive. "Maybe."

"We should do a project together," Ellen suggested.

"You should, Laurel," Jack declared. "Maybe you'd win a prize."

The science talk must have bored Ashley because she changed the subject. "We were just talking about ski season," she said, giving Jack's arm a possessive hug. "I bought a new ski outfit in Kittery the other day, and I can't wait for the snow. Do you ski, Laurel?"

"A little. I'm not very good."

"She likes to do other things," Jack put in loyally. "Canoeing, bird-watching . . ."

Ashley laughed. "You'd rather look at birds than ski?"

Luckily we'd reached the room where the science club meets, so I didn't have to answer her. "So long," Jack said as he and Ashley continued on toward the gym.

Ellen and I sat down. "Ashley's something else," she commented.

"You're not kidding."

"Jack must have a split personality. He's best friends with you, and he's dating her. You two are like different species. What's the common denominator?"

Personally, I thought that Jack going out with Ashley Esposito was pretty depressing, but Ellen's expression was so genuinely baffled, I had to laugh. "Beats me."

November days are short. It was already dusk when I got home from the science club meeting. Still in my parka and mittens, I let Snickers out of her crate, clipped her leash to her collar, and took her outside for a walk.

This was my favorite part of the day. It's hard to explain, but I always feel really connected to animals, and that was especially true with Snickers. Walking with her was my time to just be.

As we crossed the street to the park it started to snow—big fat flakes that made Snickers bark and jump. It was the first snow of the year.

"What do you think?" I asked as she snapped at a snowflake, trying to eat it. "Cold, huh?"

I let her off the leash so she could romp a little. The snow was falling faster. I tilted back my head. Flakes stung my cheeks and nose—I opened my mouth to get a taste.

As snowflakes tickled my tongue I almost smiled. Then I remembered . . . not that I could ever forget. One month since she died, I thought. A month that had felt like a year, each hour heavy and dark.

I clapped my mittened hands together, whistling for Snickers, but she was busy digging a hole and didn't pay attention to me. The snow swirled around us, and suddenly I was bombarded by the kinds of memories I'd been trying hard lately to suppress. Daisy had loved winter. We'd always had so much fun playing in the snow! She made the goofiest snowmen—there'd been one with a baseball mitt and Boston Red Sox cap. And she never got tired of towing me and Lily on the sled up the hill in our old backyard on Lighthouse Road. Then there was that big neighborhood snowball fight when I was about seven. Kyle Cooper had nailed me in the nose. Daisy made sure I was okay and then carried me home piggyback.

Tears streamed down my face, mingling with melted snowflakes. "Snickers, come on," I shouted hoarsely.

I started walking home. Then the walk turned into a run. I could hardly see where I was going, and I didn't even care if Snickers was following me, which luckily she was. I ran blindly down Main Street, back to my building and up the stairs, with Snickers barking at my heels because she thought this was some sort of new game.

"Hello?" I cried out when I entered the apartment. Silence answered me. "Mom?"

No one was home.

At that moment I would have welcomed even Lily's company. *Where are they?* I wondered, shivering uncontrollably.

I stood in the kitchen, still bundled in my parka. My frantic gaze came to rest on the telephone. Quickly I grabbed the handset and punched in a well-known telephone number. "You're home from wrestling," I exclaimed with relief when I heard Jack's voice.

"What's wrong, Laurel?"

"Oh, Jack." A sob caught in my throat.

I started to cry. "Are you at home?" he asked.

"Yes."

"I'll be right over."

Five minutes later car tires screeched to a stop in front of the bakery. Jack's feet pounded on the stairs and he pushed through the front door, which I'd left ajar. "Oh, Laurel," he said. I was too sad to be embarrassed about bawling in front of him—not that I could have stopped. "Here, let's get you out of that coat."

He unzipped my parka and pulled it off, draping it over a chair. I'd hoped that seeing him would cheer me up, but somehow his tenderness only made me cry harder. "Jack, I can't stand it anymore," I sobbed, flinging myself into his arms.

"I know," he said, hugging me.

"Why did it have to happen to *her*, when so many people loved her?"

"It doesn't seem fair."

"I want her back."

"I know."

Jack kept murmuring comforting things as he stroked my hair.

I clung to him tightly. I knew that if I let go, I'd start to fall over that cliff that always seemed to be right in front of me these days. "Oh, Jack," I whispered. "What would I do without you?"

I lifted my tear-streaked face to his. In my grief, I hadn't really noticed how close we were, but now

I grew aware of the warmth of his body against mine. I stared into the green eyes I knew so well. "Jack," I whispered again.

I'm not sure if I made the first move or if he did, but suddenly my mouth touched his and we were kissing. It was galaxies apart from our awkward spin-the-bottle kiss back in eighth grade. It was an adult kiss—deep, searching, passionate.

I wanted it to last forever.

Six

"You might as well just shoot me," I told Ellen as we huddled by my locker the next morning, "before I die of embarrassment."

"I can't believe you guys *kissed.*" Ellen grabbed my arm and gave it a shake. "After knowing each other for, like, a hundred *years!* And when he's dating *Ashley!* What happened after that?"

I filled Ellen in on the rest of the episode, including Lily's timely arrival. Jack and I hadn't gotten a chance to talk about the kiss, and when he called later, I instructed Lily to tell him I was asleep.

Now I considered climbing into my locker and locking the door behind me. "I only told you because we might need to make a speedy getaway," I explained. "In case we see—"

At that moment I spotted Jack striding purposefully toward me. Slamming my locker, I bolted in the opposite direction, Ellen hurrying after me. At the end of the corridor I ducked into the girls' room. "How long do you think you can keep this up?" she panted.

"Indefinitely," I replied.

Avoiding Jack was a challenge, though. We

usually sat next to each other in the second-to-last row in English. Today I slipped into class just as the bell was ringing, snagging the last empty seat in the front row. I could feel Jack's eyes on the back of my head for the whole hour, but when the bell rang at the end of class, I sprinted out of the room before he could catch me.

I knew I'd be a sitting duck in the cafeteria, so I decided to spend lunch period in the library. I took a roundabout route, steering way clear of Jack's locker. Just when I thought I was safe, though, I rounded a corner and bumped right into him.

"Whoa." Before I could try the girls' room trick again, Jack grabbed my arm. "Hold on."

"I have to go. There's a book in the library I really—"

"We need to talk," he cut in.

My face was burning. When I saw that Jack's was pink, too, I blushed even harder. "What if we just pretend this whole thing—"

Still holding my arm, he dragged me over to the stairwell door. "No."

I was trapped, so as soon as we were alone in the stairwell, I launched into the speech I'd been rehearsing in my head all morning. "About yesterday," I began. "I was just upset. It was a mistake. Ashley doesn't have to know anything about it. I'm really sorry—"

"I'm not," Jack interrupted.

I blinked at him. "You're not?"

He shook his head, smiling wryly. "Are you kidding? That was a great kiss."

My blush had started to fade, but now my cheeks flamed again. It *was* a great kiss, I had to admit. Not that I had much to compare it to, but still, I'd read enough books and seen enough movies. "But Jack. You and me. We're friends."

"We're friends," he agreed. His eyes were shining with a bright, hungry light. "But that's not all, at least, not for me. I've been in love with you a long time, Laurel."

In *love?* "B-But in j-junior high, w-we—"

"That going-steady fiasco—yeah, I remember. You wanted to be just friends after that, so I hid my feelings. But they didn't change."

I was speechless. Not that Jack's words should have totally surprised me—on some level, deep inside, I could have guessed how he felt about me. "But what about Ashley?" I asked.

"Forget Ashley," Jack said gruffly.

"But you're a couple."

He shrugged. "We're not serious."

I didn't get it. Ashley was gorgeous—half the boys in our class had a crush on her. "How *come* you're not serious?"

"I don't love her. I love *you*, and I always have."

Jack stepped over and slipped his arms around my waist, pulling me close. "She's so pretty, though," I said, resisting the hug a little.

"Not where it counts."

"She's a cheerleader! Everybody wants to go out with a cheerleader."

"Yeah, but she doesn't know the names of the constellations and she can't climb a tree and she couldn't tell bear tracks from coyote tracks. She doesn't think about things the way you do. She doesn't *care* about things the way you do."

Relaxing a little, I allowed Jack to hold me. I still felt self-conscious, but it was passing. This feels okay, I thought. "I still don't understand. If you don't like Ashley, why have you been hanging out with her?"

"I don't know. I was a little mad at you, I guess. I felt like you took me for granted. Okay, I'm not proud of this, but I wanted to make you jealous."

"I *was* jealous," I admitted. It was true, even though the jealousy hadn't felt romantic. Or had it? I was confused.

"But then, after Daisy died, spending time with Ashley started to feel wrong. I was thinking about breaking up with her. Not that you gave me any encouragement in that direction." He gave me a squeeze. "That is, until yesterday."

"You're going to break up?"

"Yes."

I didn't try to talk him out of it. Let's face it, I wanted Jack all to myself. "What do we do now?" I asked.

"I have a proposal," Jack said.

"What?"

"We could kiss again. Then if it *was* a mistake, like back in eighth grade, we'll know. Right?"

It sounded logical. I smiled. "Right."

"All right. So, um . . ." He put his hand under my chin, tipping my face upward. "Is this . . . okay?"

I didn't answer. I didn't have to. We kissed for a long time, and it wasn't like eighth grade at all. It was awesome—even better than the day before.

There was something else about this kiss. This time it wasn't an accident. We knew what we were doing, so it felt like a promise. Like the start of something.

Me and Jack, I thought dizzily. Me and Jack!

"You and Jack. Cool," said Karlee Kennedy, who's in my homeroom.

That pretty much seemed to be everyone's opinion. By lunchtime on Wednesday the whole school knew that Jack and Ashley had broken up and that Ashley was now going out with Reeve Shipley, cocaptain of the South Regional varsity ice hockey team, and that Jack and I were a couple. In some ways being a couple was totally weird, but in other ways it felt completely normal. It was distracting, anyhow. It gave me something to think about besides Daisy.

"I saw you holding hands in the hall!" Ellen hissed in my ear as we walked into physics.

She and I had gotten pretty tight lately. It was

kind of fun to have a girlfriend to gossip with. "So?" I hissed back, only blushing a little.

"So, I still can't believe it."

I shrugged. I'd never had a boyfriend to hold hands with in the hall, unless you counted my brief nonrelationship with Nathan Green in eighth grade, but now that I did, it really didn't seem like that big a deal. "It's just Jack," I reminded Ellen.

"Yeah, but things are different now," she pointed out.

Maybe that was true, but in some ways nothing had changed. Jack was still my best friend. It was kind of convenient, really. "I always thought I'd be nervous about going out with somebody," I confided. "I wouldn't know what to say or how to act. But it's not like that at all with Jack."

"I'm psyched for you guys," Ellen said. "I always thought you'd make a great couple."

"You did? You could have predicted this?"

Ellen nodded wisely. "Of *course*. It was *inevitable*."

I bounced Ellen's theory off Jack as we waited for the movie to start at the cinema in Kent on Friday night. "Do you think this was inevitable?" I asked, reaching over for a handful of popcorn.

Jack slid an arm across the back of my seat. "Yep."

"You mean, like, destiny?"

He flashed me a grin. "Definitely. Destiny. Meant to be. I didn't even mind having to wait for you. Like Meredith in the meadow."

The lights dimmed and the previews started. We finished the popcorn, and Jack put the empty box on the floor so he could take my hand. He leaned over to whisper in my ear, "You're not getting cold feet, are you?"

My feet were pretty warm, and so was the rest of me. "I don't think so," I whispered back.

We didn't get home until almost midnight. "This is the first time I've stayed out until my curfew," I told Jack as he parked in front of Wissinger's Bakery. "I wonder if Mom's waiting up for me?"

"She knows you're in good hands," Jack said.

We unbuckled our seat belts and then sat there. Time to make out, I thought nervously. "Um, do you want to . . ."

"Yes," said Jack.

"Okay. So . . . how?"

"Like this," he suggested, pulling me close.

I was halfway on his lap, with the gearshift poking me in the waist. I felt pretty ridiculous. After kissing for a minute I pulled back. "Does this seem kind of . . . um . . . *physical* to you?" I asked, figuring Jack might as well know what was on my mind. "Since this is only our first real date?"

"You mean, maybe we shouldn't be kissing when we hardly know each other?" he joked.

"Seriously," I said. "Maybe it was inevitable and all that, but that doesn't mean we have to go so fast."

"I won't pressure you about sex," he promised.

"I'd never be like that, especially not with you."

"Good. But Jack . . ."

His eyes twinkled in the darkness. "Unless you *want* me to pressure you about sex."

"No!" Just the mention of the word *sex* made me blush furiously. "What I'm trying to say is . . ." I hesitated. What *was* I trying to say? How *did* I feel about all of this? "It's me, Jack. Laurel Walker, the girl who used to make you roll up your nice pants and wade around in mud puddles collecting tadpoles. Is this really what you're looking for?"

Jack's arms tightened around me. "Didn't I tell you that I've always been crazy about you?"

I squirmed a little. "Yeah, but—"

"I'm not going back to before," he said suddenly.

"You're not?"

"We're not," he corrected himself. "This is better. Isn't it?"

I gazed into his eyes. They were so warm and loving. Just then I realized something. I hadn't cried once today, and it was thanks to Jack. Who could ask for a more perfect boyfriend? He knew me better than anyone else. He knew what I was going through. And he'd help me deal with it. Maybe I'd be okay after all. "Yes," I said softly. "It's better."

We kissed again. Jack was a great kisser—a lot better than me, I'm sure. His kisses made me feel as if we were the only two people on the planet.

"I adore you," he whispered in my ear.

I snuggled into the curve of Jack's arm. No one had ever said that to me, and if I'd thought about it, I might have been embarrassed. But I didn't think about it. It was easier just to feel, and at that moment I felt better than I had in a long time.

Seven

The next morning Lily talked Mom into taking us to a wedding reception she was catering at an oceanfront mansion a few miles up the coast. Mom didn't have much choice—the night before, Sarah had come down with a bad case of the flu. I was pretty sure Lily didn't actually plan to work—she probably just wanted to mingle with the guests and pretend she was someone she's not—but I intended to be as helpful as possible. Who knows? I thought, not quite daring to hope. Maybe I'd do a great job! Anyway, some experience with wedding stuff would probably be good for me—I could use a little maid of honor practice.

The first hour Lily and I set tables on the veranda. Then, while Mom consulted with the florist and the bartender, we started warming up hors d'oeuvres—the huge kitchen had four ovens. Mom always made giant batches of appetizers ahead of time and kept them frozen until the day of the party.

We could hear the guests beginning to arrive. Mom stuck her head in the kitchen. "When the first tray is ready, bring it out," she told me before disappearing again.

"I can't believe *you're* going out with Jack Harrison," Lily remarked, using a hot mitt to pull a baking sheet from the oven. "He's so cool and you're so . . . not."

"What do you know about anything?" I retorted. I started arranging the little shrimp and goat cheese tarts on a silver platter. "Here." I tossed Lily a dish towel. "Wash those other platters—they got dusty in the car. I'm going to pass out the hors d'oeuvres."

"Why should *I* wash the platters?" Lily protested. "I want to pass hors d'oeuvres."

I was trying to be patient with her but having a hard time. "Because I'm the oldest and Mom wants me to do it." I picked up the tray.

"You are the least coordinated and graceful person in the entire world," Lily declared. "I'm going to pass the hors d'oeuvres. I'll do a much better job." She tried to take the tray from me.

I pulled it back. "No, you're not."

"Yes, I am."

She gave the tray a yank and it slipped out of my hands. The next thing we knew, the tray flew into the air and suddenly it was raining shrimp tarts! "Now look what you did!" I cried.

Of course Mom had to pick that moment to come back into the kitchen with a tray of empty champagne glasses. When she saw hors d'oeuvres all over the floor, she flushed angrily. "What's going on here?"

"I'm sorry, Mom," I whispered.

"It was Laurel's fault," Lily said. "She's making me do all the grunt work."

Mom swept the ruined food into a garbage bag. "You're lucky I brought extra appetizers," she snapped. "There's a Ziploc bag with mushroom toasts in the freezer, Laurel. And if there's any more fighting between the two of you, you're both going home. Do you understand me?"

"Yes," Lily and I mumbled.

Mom went back out to the party. I scowled at Lily and she scowled back at me. "I can't believe you did that," I said. I was so mad and ashamed, I felt like crying. "You messed up my chance to do a good job for Mom."

"*I* messed up your chance?" Lily scoffed. "You're lucky I saved you from spilling those appetizers all over the wedding guests."

"Oh, just wash the platters," I said. "I'll put the mushroom toasts in the oven. You can pass them out when they're warm."

Lily ended up passing out appetizers the whole time while I worked in the kitchen. She had a blast. I was miserable. Driving home after the reception, Mom pulled the car over to the side of the road and apologized. "Accidents happen," she said. "I shouldn't have come down so hard on you two. I was just feeling stressed. Will you forgive me?"

"Of course, Mom," I said.

"Don't worry about it," Lily agreed.

Mom didn't bring it up again. She also didn't

ask me to help her with the next party she catered or the one after that. Big surprise.

When I mentioned it, she said it was only because she didn't want to put pressure on me. "This family's going through a hard time," she said. "Let's not rock the boat, okay? Just have fun with Jack."

"Sure, Mom." I knew what she was really thinking, though. Come out of your shell, people are always urging me. Don't be so shy. Well, I'd had a chance to follow in Daisy's footsteps and I'd tripped all over myself. I belonged in my shell, where I wouldn't look like a fool.

It almost didn't matter that Mom didn't want me to help at her parties because being part of a couple was starting to take up all my free time. Jack and I had always hung out together a lot, but now we were inseparable. During the week we met at my locker in the morning, walked each other to class, and sat together at lunch. In the evening we had study dates. Then every Friday and Saturday night we went out. Jack had lots of friends, so there was almost always a party to go to. Before we started dating, I never went to parties—I could never think of anything to say to people I didn't know well. Even after we started going out and I kind of became a regular on the junior class party scene, I always stuck close to Jack and let him do most of the talking.

"What's up tonight?" I asked him one Friday morning in December as we walked to homeroom. We'd been dating for three weeks. "We don't have to go out if there's nothing special going on."

"I kind of assumed we would." Jack looked hurt that I'd even suggested otherwise. "Don't you want to?"

"I didn't say I didn't want to. I just meant, you know, we don't *have* to just because it's Friday." I skipped a beat. "Or do we?"

Jack draped an arm around my shoulders. "Of course we don't *have* to. There's no law. Like I said, it's only if you want to. You do, don't you?"

"Sure," I said.

"Maybe we can double with Eric and Monica," Jack suggested. Eric was his best wrestling team buddy; Monica was Eric's girlfriend.

"Okay," I said.

And that was that. We had another date. I couldn't exactly complain about it even though the plan didn't thrill me. After Jack kissed me good-bye outside my homeroom, I glimpsed a bunch of freshmen girls ogling me enviously. They started to whisper, and I knew what they were saying: "She's so lucky to be Jack Harrison's girlfriend!"

I *am* lucky, I thought. Not only was Jack cute, he was thoughtful, chivalrous, funny, and sweet. He dressed nicely and got good grades. He drove a funky car. He lived in a beautiful house with really cool parents. Best of all, he loved me.

When we first got together, Jack had said that I used to take him for granted. I knew I'd never do that again.

* * *

We had a pretty good time at the movies with Eric and Monica on Friday. Saturday morning I found a message from Mom—Ellen had called the night before. I decided to call her back before having breakfast and heading to the WRC. Maybe she'd want to meet me at the center for lunch—we needed to talk about possible science fair projects.

I was about to pick up the receiver when it rang right under my hand. "Hello?" I said.

"Hi, Laurel," Jack said.

"Hi. What's up?"

"I just wanted to touch base with you about the skating party this afternoon," he told me. "It turns out it's at four, not three. I guess Karlee's family has floodlights at their pond."

"See you at four, then."

"And I was thinking about something else," Jack went on. "You know the science fair at school?"

"Ellen and I have been total slouches," I confessed. "We haven't even started yet."

"Good, because I want to be your partner," Jack said.

"What?"

"Your partner," he repeated. "Wouldn't that be fun?"

I sat down at the kitchen table, the phone cradled between my shoulder and ear, and adjusted one of the straps on my overalls. "Well . . ."

"I already have an idea. Tell me how this sounds."

He described a software program he wanted to

write—a cross between a science tutorial and an adventure game. "Computers aren't my thing," I reminded him.

"Well, I'll do whatever you want to do, then," Jack replied. "You're the science whiz. All I want to do is find a way for us to spend more time together."

Personally, I didn't see how that would be possible, but I didn't say so. "The thing is, I already told Ellen I'd work with her," I told him.

"She won't mind if you work with me instead."

"I'm just not sure I want to—"

"I'll ask her, then," he said. "Call you right back."

He hung up. I dialed Ellen's number. It was busy. I have to admit that I was somewhat relieved that Ellen didn't have call waiting. I wasn't sure how I felt about the whole situation—angry that Jack was being so presumptuous or flattered that he liked me so much?

Three minutes later, as I was pouring milk on my cornflakes, the phone rang again. "It's all set," Jack announced. "You and I can be partners— Ellen said she doesn't mind flying solo."

"But what about what *I* want?" I asked.

"What do you mean? We want the same thing, right?"

I wasn't really sure *what* I wanted, so I tried another angle. "Are you sure you have time for it? You've already got wrestling, and I thought you wanted to get a weekend job at the realtor's or the travel agency."

"I've changed my mind about that," Jack told me. "I'd rather spend time with you."

I wrinkled my forehead. "Really?"

"Really. I love you, Laurel."

I hesitated for a second. Jack's voice was full of an emotion. I wasn't sure I entirely understood.

"Laurel?"

"Uh, I love you, too," I said quickly. "I do," I added, in case I hadn't sounded convincing enough the first time.

"Good. See you at four."

"Bye."

I hung up the receiver and stared at my soggy cornflakes. My head was spinning a little. I guess it's good that Jack knows more about this relationship stuff than I do, I thought, so he can tell me how things are supposed to work.

I felt as if I didn't have a clue.

I left work at the WRC a little early so I'd have time to change before the skating party. Overalls and a turtleneck or leggings and a sweater? I wondered, staring into my closet.

Lily broke into my train of thought. "It's a good day for it," she announced, sticking her head into my bedroom.

"A good day for what?" I asked.

"For cutting down a Christmas tree," she answered. "Mom's got a job in Portland, but Hal said he'd drive us to McCloskey's in the Subaru to pick one out."

Maybe the other girls at the party would be wearing perky skating outfits, but I decided to stick with overalls since I was already wearing them. "I don't think so," I said to my sister.

"What don't you think?"

I turned around to look at her. "I don't think it's a good day to get a tree."

She strolled into the room and stuck a finger between the bars of the birdcage to stroke Clark's feathers. "When do you want to go, then?"

"Maybe I don't. Not this year."

I didn't explain myself further, but it had to be obvious what I meant. *Not this year, without Daisy.*

"But I want to cut down a tree the way we always have," Lily whined.

"Go with Hal, then. I don't have time."

Clark gave Lily's finger a peck. She jumped away from the cage, tears springing into her eyes. "Did he hurt you?" I asked worriedly.

She shook her head. "No."

"Then why are you—" I sighed. Clearly this meant a lot to Lily. Still, the idea of going to get a tree without Daisy . . . Get over it, I told myself sternly. You'll have to get a tree sooner or later. "Okay," I said, relenting. "I only have half an hour, though, so let's get going."

As it turned out, Hal didn't have time to take us after all. He'd gotten called into the office to do some work for a client who was being audited by the IRS—he was on his way out the door. "Take the car," he said, tossing me the keys. I had my license by then.

"Are you sure you don't need it?"

He nodded, smiling. "The office is only a block away. I think I can walk."

With Lily in the passenger seat I drove slowly out the Old Boston Post Road to McCloskey's Farm. "You're a good driver," Lily ventured after a minute. "You know, always using your turn signals and stuff."

I still didn't have that much experience behind the wheel, so I was cautious. "Mom hardly ever lets me drive," I remarked.

"Because of Daisy's accident," Lily said simply.

"Oh." I hadn't really thought about it. "Right."

We were quiet the rest of the way to McCloskey's. Since we didn't have much time, we decided to take a ready-cut tree instead of cutting one down ourselves the way we always did in the old days. It wouldn't have been any fun, anyway, without Rose and Mom singing Christmas carols, and without Daisy. She'd always been the one who spotted the perfect tree.

Mr. McCloskey helped us tie the tree to the roof of the Subaru with twine. I was climbing into the driver's seat when Lily trotted back to the farm stand. "One more thing," she called.

When she got in the car, she was holding two small evergreen wreaths decorated with berries and ribbon. "What are those for?" I asked.

"You'll see," she replied.

Driving back to town, we passed the cemetery. "Stop," Lily commanded.

"Here?"

"Yeah. Park by the church."

I guessed what she had in mind. I followed her into the cemetery and watched as she laid one wreath on Daisy's grave and the other by Dad's headstone. "I know you're in a hurry," she said, glancing at me over her shoulder. "Can we just take a minute?"

"Sure," I said. Suddenly I didn't care about getting to the skating party on time. "As long as you want."

She sat down on the dry brown grass. "I come here a lot," she confessed.

"Really?"

She nodded. "I talk to Dad and Daisy." Lily cast me a sideways glance. "I guess that sounds kind of weird."

I shrugged. "I don't know. Do they . . . do they talk back?"

"No. But sometimes I feel like they're close by."

We both fell silent. The wind whispered in the pines, reminding me of Lily's funeral poem.

Finally Lily sighed long and deep. "Let's go," she said.

When we got home, I parked Hal's car in front of our building. "We can take the tree off later. Would you drop the keys through Hal's mail slot?" I asked Lily. "I'm going to wait down here for Jack."

Lily lingered on the sidewalk with me. "You're going to a skating party, huh?"

"Yep."

"I love skating."

"I know."

"I just bought this vintage velvet skating skirt at Second Time Around. It's really cute and swirly."

"Hmmm."

"Can I come with you?"

I shook my head. "It's going to be all juniors. You wouldn't know anyone."

Lily clasped her hands. "Please?"

Was she kidding? "It's a *date*, Lil. Two's company, you know?"

Lily didn't get a chance to beg further because Jack pulled up. I hopped into the Mustang and waved good-bye. I know it sounds awful, but I couldn't wait to get away from her suddenly. The whole Christmas tree excursion had made me so . . . sad. Skating with Jack would take my mind off all that. "See you later," I told her.

As we drove off, I looked in the side mirror. Lily was still standing on the sidewalk, watching us go. Maybe Lily's like me, I thought, beginning to feel bad about leaving her behind. She just doesn't like to be alone these days.

We were too far away now for me to see the expression in my sister's eyes, though. And when Jack turned the corner, Lily disappeared from sight.

I forgot all about Lily when we got to Karlee's house. Jack is Mr. Winter Sports, but I'm not a good skater, and even with him holding my hand, I had to struggle to stay upright on the frozen pond in the Kennedys' backyard. "This isn't natural," I said. "Balancing on these skinny blades. I like having my feet flat on the ground."

Jack swept me in a circle, then twirled me—shrieking—under his arm, Ice Capades style. "You don't give yourself enough credit."

I collapsed against him. "I'm a menace to the safety of others. Can we stop, please?"

It was getting dark and cold. We weren't the only ones who'd given up on the ice—in Karlee's basement rec room a bunch of people were drinking hot chocolate and eating sugar cookies. Jack went upstairs to the bathroom, and I had a moment of panic. Who was I going to talk to? Then I spotted Jon Rotner, a guy I knew from science club. He was standing in the corner, looking as out of place as I felt. "Hi, Jon," I said, joining him.

"Hi, Laurel," he replied with obvious relief. "Hey, I've been meaning to ask you. You work at the Wildlife Rescue Center, right? Are they looking for any volunteers these days?"

I started telling Jon about how Griffin wanted the center to get involved in more educational outreach programs. I was really pleased that Jon wanted to help out—we could definitely use it. Our conversation got pretty intense, so when someone hugged me from behind, I jumped. Of course it was Jack, but for a second I must have forgotten we were a couple. I almost shouted, "What do you think you're *doing?*" Luckily I remembered in time and smiled at him instead.

"Laurel, can you move over a little?" Jack requested politely but mysteriously. "Take, like, three steps sideways?"

I raised my eyebrows. "Why?"

"Just do it," he said, grinning.

I took a couple of steps with Jack hovering over me. When I stopped, he leaned in and gave me a big kiss on the lips. "Jack!" I exclaimed, blushing.

He pointed upward. "Mistletoe."

I twisted around to apologize to Jon for ditching him, but he'd already melted back into the crowd. Meanwhile Jack started to kiss me again. Suddenly I felt claustrophobic. "Let's go back outside," I said abruptly.

"I thought you weren't into skating."

"I feel like some fresh air. Okay?"

"Sure." Jack slid his hands up my arms and playfully flicked the straps on my overalls. For some reason, it made me want to smack him. "No problem."

We bundled up again and went outside, and Jack immediately got pulled into a twilight game of touch football. I sat down on a nearby tree stump, pushing my hands deep into the pockets of my parka. Jack was good at running and passing and being part of a team. There was a lot of laughter and high-fiving. Gradually the closed-in feeling I'd had inside Karlee's house faded. The evening air smelled like pine needles and wood smoke and snow. I like being by myself like this, I realized, more than I like being at parties.

Immediately I felt disloyal. It wasn't that I didn't like having a boyfriend and a social life, I told myself. I did, and I figured I'd get better at it as time passed. I just needed my own space. I'd always been that way. That was why I'd liked Jack so much when we first met when we were ten. I was this shy, odd kid who liked to mess around in the woods or sit in a hammock with a book, and he didn't seem to mind that we didn't talk that much. He hadn't had so many friends back then.

"Touchdown!" Jack shouted, doing a little dance on the far side of the yard. He looked over at me for approval.

I remembered to act like a girlfriend. "Way to go!" I yelled, clapping.

Eight

"The house looks beautiful," Rose told Mom on Christmas Eve.

"We threw the decorations up at the last minute," Mom confessed.

Rose had gotten home from Boston just that day, after finishing her finals at BU. The four of us were in the living room now, dressed for church despite the fact that it was snowing like crazy outside and the roads would be terrible. Snickers, who was four months old now, was on the couch with me, her head on my lap.

Rose, Lily, and I watched as Mom unpacked the Christmas stockings and hung them from hooks on the mantel. "Rose's stocking is bigger than mine," Lily pouted.

I rolled my eyes. "You say that every year."

"And then you count your stocking presents to make sure you didn't get shortchanged," Rose put in.

"So?" Lily asked. "Why shouldn't I?"

Usually when Lily says something like that, Mom tells her not to be so greedy. Now, though, Mom remained quiet. She was standing by the fireplace, her head bent, holding something. Daisy's

Christmas stocking, I realized, my heart swelling with sorrow.

Rose went over to Mom and put an arm around her. "Are you okay?" she asked softly.

Mom nodded. Bending, she laid the stocking carefully back in the box, covering it with tissue paper. "Every now and then something takes me by surprise," she said in a small voice. "I have some piece of her in my hand and I simply can't believe she's gone."

We were all quiet for a minute. I scratched Snickers's silky ears, my eyes on the snow whirling beyond the windowpanes. Lily sniffled. Sadness filled the room, but before the real tears could start, the colored lights on the Christmas tree flickered and then the room went dark.

"The power's out!" Lily exclaimed.

This kind of thing happens a couple of times a year, and we jumped into action. Rose got out the candles while I hunted for matches. Flashlight in hand, Mom went into the kitchen to check that the gas stove was still working—she was toasting bread cubes for the turkey stuffing. "Should I put another log on the fire so the room stays warm?" Lily asked.

"Not if we're still going to church," Rose replied. "Are we, Mom?"

"I think we should," Mom answered.

"But won't the power be out there, too?" I asked.

"Maybe," Mom said. "But it's Christmas Eve.

Reverend Beecher would hardly cancel services."

Mom was right, of course. The little church was packed, and people kept their coats on and sang carols by candlelight. "I really feel the Christmas spirit," Rose whispered to me after the congregation sang "Silent Night." "Don't you, Laurel?"

I nodded.

I did feel the Christmas spirit, although it was more solemn than joyful.

The next morning the electricity came back on, and the sun sparkled on new snow. Delicious smells drifted from the kitchen, and there were plenty of presents to open—homemade gifts, mostly, because that became our tradition after Dad died. But when Rose tried to snap some pictures with the new camera Stephen had given her, it was hard for any of us to smile. Memories of Daisy were too vivid.

When Christmas dinner was ready, we gathered in the dining room. Mom stood behind her chair at the foot of the table, with Hal at the head. Even with Stephen there, one spot was empty. I tried not to look at it, but I saw Lily's eyes dart in that direction. "Why don't you say grace?" Mom asked Hal.

We stood around the table, holding one another's hands, our heads bowed. "Gracious God, help us be thankful for our many blessings," Hal began.

Before he could continue, Lily burst into tears. "Excuse me," she sobbed, running from the room.

Rose and Mom went after Lily. Unsure what to do, I turned to look at Stephen. He was standing to my right, and our hands were still clasped. He gave mine a squeeze. "It's tough, isn't it?" he said simply. I nodded, not trusting myself to speak. I didn't let go of his hand.

Mom and Rose returned. Hal walked over and rested a comforting hand on Mom's shoulder. "Let's eat," she said quietly. "Lily said she'd join us in a few minutes."

Lily didn't come back to the table, though, and the rest of us ate in silence. Gracious God, I found myself praying, help us be thankful for our many blessings. Even with Daisy gone, I knew I *did* have a lot to be thankful for. My family was loving and strong. I still had two sisters and the world's best mother. Hal was really supportive to all of us. And I had Jack.

A strange longing washed over me. Jack was coming over with his parents for dessert, and suddenly I couldn't wait to see him. There were some aspects of being in a relationship that I still hadn't adjusted to, but I knew one thing for sure. When my grief over Daisy was the worst, being with Jack was the only thing that seemed to help.

"We're doing the rehearsal dinner at the Harborside, and Stephen's parents have offered to have the reception at their house," Rose said to Mom. It was the morning after Christmas, and they were discussing wedding plans over coffee in the kitchen. "They have that big backyard with the gardens—we can set up a tent."

"How many people do you want to invite?" Mom asked, pouring fresh coffee into her and Rose's cups.

"Eighty or a hundred." Rose looked at me, wrinkling her nose. "Does that sound absolutely huge, Laurel?"

I sat down with a bowl of oatmeal. "I don't know."

"Because the thing is, Stephen has about a million cousins and he wants to invite them all," Rose went on. "And when we start adding up all our friends . . ."

"You only have one wedding," Lily put in. She was toasting an English muffin. "You should be able to invite everyone you want."

Mom drummed her fingers on the tabletop in a thoughtful way. "Lily's right. We'll keep costs down by doing as much as possible ourselves."

"Cath's dad told me he can get rental stuff, like tables and chairs and tents, for a discount," Rose said. "And some friends of mine from BU who are in a band will do the music."

"And I'll do the food," Mom said.

Rose raised her eyebrows. "How can you do the food? You're the mother of the bride!"

Mom laughed. "You'll pitch in, of course, and we'll have Sarah. It will be something for you to do the day before the wedding so you don't get too jittery."

"Why would I be jittery?" Rose smiled. "I'm marrying my best friend."

Mom's eyes got misty. We all cry at the drop of a hat these days. "Oh, honey. I'm so glad. That's exactly what marriage should be about."

I finished my oatmeal as fast as I could. Mom and Rose were acting like they were in one of those corny coffee commercials. I mean, I was dating *my* best friend, but it didn't make me all dewy eyed. "Wait, Laurel," Rose said when I pushed back my chair. "I want your advice about clothes."

"Clothes?" I repeated, as surprised as if she'd said "mutual funds."

"Stephen and I aren't sure whether to go the formal route—you know, long white gown, tuxedo—or to wear something more casual. What do you think?"

"You're asking the wrong person," Lily interjected before I could answer. "Laurel has no fashion sense."

Rose shushed Lily. "I'd like Laurel's opinion."

"I don't know," I said.

"I'm just not sure," Rose confided. "I always fantasized about a lacy white princess dress with a long veil, but it could be cool to wear something more sophisticated." She gave me a hopeful smile. "What kind of bridesmaid dress do you want?"

"I'll wear whatever you want me to wear," I replied.

Rose turned to Mom. "I told Laurel about the bridal shower."

"I'll be happy to help you plan it when the time comes, Laurel," Mom offered.

"Someone else should probably be in charge," I said.

"Why?" Rose wanted to know.

"Mom can tell you about the spilled hors d'oeuvres," I explained. "If you leave it up to me, it'll be a disaster."

"What spilled hors d'oeuvres?" Rose asked.

"That was an accident," Mom remarked. "The shower will be fine."

"It's not too late to make *me* your maid of honor, Rose," Lily kidded. "Or at least your style consultant. Can we look at those bridal magazines you bought the other day?"

While Rose went for the magazines, I made my escape. I didn't feel like talking about the wedding. When Rose and Stephen had first announced their engagement back in October, I'd been really psyched. Now, for some reason, I couldn't deal with it at all.

Maybe it's because Rose expects me to take Daisy's place, I thought. And I knew I never could.

Mr. and Mrs. Harrison throw a huge New Year's Eve party every year at their house, Windy Ridge. This year Lily had another party to go to, but my mother went to the Harrisons' with Hal, Rose took Stephen, and of course I was there to be with Jack.

"You look incredibly pretty," Jack told me as we stood in the front hall. Taking both my hands, he gave me a kiss on the cheek. "I like that dress."

Rose had loaned me the dress. It was a lot sexier

than anything I'd ever worn before——I didn't feel totally comfortable revealing so much skin. "Thanks,"
I said.

The dining and living rooms were packed with
adults, so Jack and I headed back to the library,
where kids our age were listening to music. "It's
kind of noisy," I shouted.

"And?" he shouted back.

"Do you want to go someplace quieter?"

He wiggled his eyebrows at me. "Is this a
proposition?"

"Could be."

We ended up in his bedroom. "I didn't think
I'd get you up here until the end of the party," he
joked.

"I'm just not crazy about crowds."

Jack sat down on his bed. He patted the mat-
tress next to him. "Hey, Laurel."

Instead of joining him, I wandered over to his
bookshelves. "Lloyd Alexander!" I exclaimed.
"Remember that summer when we read all the
Taran books in, like, a week?"

"The Chronicles of Narnia, too," Jack said.
"Come here."

I touched the faded spine of a well-worn vol-
ume. "*The Yearling*. I *loved* this. It was so sad."

"You always cried over the animal stories. Sit
down with me."

I shoved aside a pile of *Sports Illustrated*s to reach
Jack's photo album. I opened it up at random. "I remember this," I said, pointing to an old picture.

"Your mom and dad took us horseback riding."

"Laurel, would you come over—"

"And this one!" I tapped a page. "That Halloween when we went trick-or-treating dressed as a goalpost. Remember how hard it was to walk?"

Jack got to his feet. Taking the album from me, he tossed it on his desk and placed his hands on my shoulders. "I don't want to look at photo albums—I want to kiss you."

His lips touched mine. After a few seconds I turned my face away. "Is something wrong?" he asked.

"No. I just . . ."

"What?"

I shook my head. I had no idea why I felt the way I did. "I forgot what I was going to say. Um, how about some music?"

Jack put a CD on the stereo, a female vocalist we both liked. Turning off the light, he came over and wrapped his arms around me. "Let's pretend it's midnight," he whispered, his lips tickling my earlobe.

He was obviously feeling a lot more in the mood than I was. I thought I should at least make an effort to be romantic, though. It *was* New Year's Eve, after all. I lifted my face to his for a kiss.

It was a wonderful kiss . . . as always. Jack's arms tightened around me; his mouth on mine was warm and insistent. This is where it gets exciting, I thought. But instead of pleasant anticipation, I felt strangely detached.

Turning my face away again, I rested my head on Jack's shoulder. As we swayed to the music, a sigh escaped me. "I hope this is okay," I whispered.

"What?"

"That I just want to be held."

I looked up and our eyes met. Jack nodded. "I want whatever you want, Laurel."

So we slow-danced in the darkness as the final minutes of the year ticked away.

Nine

It was a gloomy January in Hawk Harbor—record amounts of snow and day after day of icy temperatures. By the end of the month I had a serious case of cabin fever. I took Snickers for short walks every morning, afternoon, and night—she didn't mind the cold—but that was about it.

Jack called one Saturday morning as I was wrapping a scarf around my neck. "Let's go to Kent for lunch and a matinee," he suggested.

"I have to work at the WRC," I reminded him.

"You're always over there." Jack's tone reminded me oddly of Lily. If he weren't my boyfriend, I'd have called it whining. "Can't you call in sick or something?"

"I suppose I could . . . but I don't want to. I like my job."

"Better than me?"

"Of course not! Don't be ridiculous. What are your other friends up to today?"

"Eric got tickets for a Celtics game."

I knew Jack liked basketball. "That's a hundred times better than seeing a movie in Kent," I pointed out.

109

"Yeah, well, I'm not going," Jack said.

"Why not?"

"I'd rather be with you."

I couldn't believe Jack would pass up live NBA in order to sit around waiting for me to get home. It was his choice, though, I supposed. "I'll see you after work, then."

"Love you, Laurel."

"Love you, too."

With a feeling of escape, I headed outside to the car. It was cold, and the engine coughed and sputtered for a few minutes before finally starting with a grouchy roar.

The snow tires made a nice, crunchy sound as I drove down Main Street, which was covered with a new layer of powder. Turning on the radio, I sang along, suddenly feeling cheerful. I *did* love my job at the WRC. It wasn't the money, although I did like watching my savings account grow. *It's the one thing I have all to myself lately,* I thought. *Jack and I do everything else together.*

"It's oppressive," I said out loud.

The words hung there in the cold air of the car. I ventured another thought out loud. "And it's driving me crazy."

It wasn't that I didn't like—rather, love—Jack, I decided as I stamped the snow off my boots outside the WRC. It *was* possible to have too much of a good thing, that was all.

Inside, Carlos was drinking some of

Griffin's *chai* tea. "We're on our own today," he informed me. "Griffin just called—his car battery's dead."

"Excuses, excuses," I kidded. "Couldn't he hitchhike or something?"

"Yeah, on the back of a snowplow." Carlos lifted his mug. "Want some?"

As we drank our tea and ate a couple of stale bran muffins I thought about how I used to be too shy around Carlos to do more than say hello. Now we talked and joked like real friends. He was definitely one of the things I liked best about the WRC.

We got to work feeding the animals and cleaning cages. Just before noon we met up by Lefty's pen. We'd worked hard on creating a good habitat, and now the baby seal had rocks to climb on and a small pool to splash around in. "Look at him," I said to Carlos. "He's getting so fat!"

"Can you believe it?" Carlos picked Lefty up. "Pretty soon he'll be too heavy to lift."

I'd already mixed up a bottle of formula. Carlos handed the seal to me. We grinned at each other. It almost felt like we were Lefty's parents or something. "You saved him," Carlos said. "Makes you feel good, doesn't it?"

I gave Lefty the bottle. He started sucking hungrily. "Yes," I said. "It makes me feel great."

"You did an incredible job."

Carlos crossed the room to take care of a wounded fox. I watched him out of the corner of my eye. An incredible job, I thought, feeling a tickle of pleasure at the compliment. Did he just say that to be nice? Probably. I wouldn't know what to do most of the time without him telling me. Then again, idle flattery wasn't really his style.

Carlos broke into my musings. "How's your science fair project coming along?" he asked, moving along to the raccoon cage.

Shifting my hold on Lefty, I grimaced. "It's not. We're doing this grafting experiment and our bean plants keep dying."

"How come?"

"I don't know." I did know, though. "Jack means well," I told Carlos, "but he doesn't have a green thumb. He doesn't—" I stopped. Carlos looked over at me. I shrugged. "We still have some time left. I'm sure it'll work out."

"Knowing you, it will," Carlos agreed.

"But I wish Ellen was my partner," I found myself confessing.

"Yeah. I would've said don't mix work and love, but maybe that's just me," Carlos remarked.

I ducked my head, brushing my chin against Lefty's soft, musky-smelling fur. I'd never really talked to Carlos about my personal life. "Anyway," I mumbled a little self-consciously.

Latching the door to the raccoon cage, Carlos started humming "Take Me Out to the Ball Game." All of a sudden, I thought of Daisy. Something about the quiet, efficient, cheerful way

Carlos went about doing things, and of course the tune he'd picked, made me see Daisy out in our old backyard, mowing the grass in the summer, her baseball cap turned backward, singing along to her Walkman. Daisy humming as she helped me with my algebra homework, or as she polished silver for Mom, or as she climbed a stepladder to put in the storm windows in the fall and then again to switch the storm windows for screens in the spring. But this time thinking about Daisy didn't make me sad, exactly. Instead it made me want to *talk*.

The words spilled from me before I even realized I was saying them out loud. "Nothing's how it should be nowadays," I blurted. "I feel like I don't know how to connect to my mom—not that she's ever around. And Lily and I might as well not even be related. All Rose thinks about is the wedding, and Jack . . . I don't know why I do *anything* anymore," I finished.

I was pretty embarrassed by this outburst, but when Carlos glanced at me, there was sympathy in his dark eyes.

He kept busy with the animals, though, as if sensing that I'd be mortified if he paid me too much attention. "You're missing Daisy, huh?" he asked.

How did he know that? I wondered, but I just nodded wordlessly, my eyes bright with tears.

"Death changes the world for the people who are left behind," he said after a minute. "I've been there, Laurel. I lost a good buddy back in high school. You're going to grieve for your sister for a long time, but eventually relationships and stuff like that will shift into a new place that feels right. You'll find your balance again."

"Really?"

"Yeah," Carlos said with quiet assurance. We looked at each other a moment. Finally I smiled, and a grin broke out over his face. "Hey, when you're done with Lefty, will you play the fishing game with the raccoon kits?"

I spent the next half hour coaching three orphaned raccoons on how to fish bits of food out of a pail of water. I got soaking wet, but they made me laugh, and at one point I caught Carlos looking at me, a half smile on his face. I wanted to thank him, but I figured I didn't need to—I was pretty sure my gratitude showed in my eyes.

Balance. A place that feels right, I thought. Maybe I'd found it already, right here.

"I don't know that much about relationships," Ellen admitted when I asked her advice the following week. "I mean, since I've never had a boyfriend. But maybe you and Jack are just in a rut. Why don't you put a little spice into your life? Do something different."

I decided Ellen was right. The way I'd been feeling about Jack lately—it wasn't that we didn't have a good relationship. The last thing I wanted was for things to go wrong between us—Jack meant the world to me. He was my anchor. We were just in a rut; that had to be the problem.

I came up with an idea for a fun, romantic outing, something I knew Jack would like. "Skiing?" he repeated when I mentioned it. We were eating lunch in the cafeteria at school. "I thought you didn't like it that much."

"Don't you think it would be fun to do something different for a change? We can drive to Cabot Mountain. We could go on a sleigh ride, too."

Jack reached over to hug me. "It'll be great," he agreed.

I got up early the following Sunday and put on long underwear under my clothes. Downstairs, I made some sandwiches and stuck them in my backpack along with a bottle of water and two apples. I was heading out the door to wait for Jack on the street when Lily came in the kitchen. "Where are you going?" she asked.

"Skiing at Cabot Mountain with Jack." Mom was in the family room, reading cookbooks. "Be home for dinner," I shouted so she could hear me.

"Cabot Mountain?" Lily's eyes lit up. "I'd love to go skiing. Can I come with you?"

I gave her the same answer I'd given the day of Karlee's skating party. "It's a date, remember?"

Lily's expression darkened. "I never get to go anywhere," she complained. "Just because I can't drive yet. It's not *fair*."

Mom walked into the room in time to hear that. "Where do you want to go, Lily?"

"Skiing with Laurel and Jack," Lily said, "but Laurel said I can't. I'm sure if I asked Jack, he'd—"

"We just don't want you tagging along, okay?" I cut in. I knew I was being rude, but I really felt like I needed this date to be as romantic as possible. And having my annoying little sister come with me was hardly going to evoke the kind of mood I was looking for.

"Maybe it's not such a bad idea, Laurel," Mom remarked, looking at me significantly.

"Yeah," Lily jumped in. "I'll run and put on my ski clothes right now." Lily raced up the stairs.

"Well, this is great," I grumbled.

"Will it really be so terrible?" Mom asked. "I'm catering a party this afternoon, so Lily would be alone all day. I'll feel a lot better if I know she's having a good time with you and Jack. Consider it a favor for me, honey."

I sighed. How could I say no to that? "Well, okay, Mom. Since you put it that way." But we're ditching her as soon as we get to the mountain, I thought as I stomped downstairs to break the news to Jack.

No such luck. Lily stuck to us like a burr. "Maybe I'll rent a snowboard," she said as we stood in line to buy lift tickets. "I've never tried it, but it looks cool. Do you know how to snowboard, Jack?"

"Yeah, it's a blast," he told her. "You'll like it."

Jack and I waited around while Lily rented a snowboard. When it looked like she was all set, I gestured to Jack. "Come on. Let's get in the lift line."

We skied over and I thought we'd finally gotten rid of Lily, but then she shouted after us, "Hey, guys, wait for me! I'll ride up with you!"

It was a quad chairlift, so we couldn't exactly blow her off, and somehow when we took our seats, she ended up in the middle. "Isn't it a beautiful day?" she asked, twisting to point at the clear blue sky and snow-dusted pine trees lining the slope. "It's not too cold. Isn't this fun?"

I rolled my eyes at Jack, but he was busy sticking his ski poles under his thigh. The whole way up the mountain Lily chattered nonstop, commenting on the outfits of the people skiing under the lift. When we dismounted at the top, Jack skied off to the right; I grabbed Lily's arm and dragged her to the left. "Look, Jack and I need to have some quality time together," I said. "We drove you here and we'll drive you home, but you can do your own thing in between, okay?"

Lily dropped onto the snow to buckle her free boot onto the board. "Fine," she agreed. "But first—"

Just then Jack skied over to us. "What's up?" he asked.

"Lily's heading over to Centennial," I said,

naming a trail on the far side of the ski area where
the snowboarders hang out.

"But first you have to tell me how to stay up on
this thing," Lily said to Jack, balancing precari-
ously on the snowboard with her arms held out.
"What do I do next?"

For the next two hours Jack gave Lily a snowboarding lesson while I skied along beside them,
flashing my little sister dirty looks, which she
cheerfully ignored. Finally Jack and I had a few
minutes alone riding up on a double chairlift. "Lily
can take care of herself, you know," I told him. "I
think we've done our duty."

"She seems to want to hang out with us,
though," Jack said. "I really don't mind."

"But this was supposed to be *romantic*," I reminded him, leaning my head on his shoulder.

"How's *this*"—Jack pushed my goggles up so he
could kiss me—"for romantic?"

From the chair behind us we heard Lily shout,
"Hey, none of that!"

Jack laughed; I groaned. "Right," I muttered.
"The pinnacle of romance."

There were plenty of kids Lily's age snowboarding and I kept hoping she'd hook up with
some of them, but no such luck. We had the
pleasure of skiing with her for the entire day.
She was starting to get the hang of snowboarding
by the time we took our last run—Jack was a
good teacher—but then she got going a little too
fast and fell. "Wow!" Jack exclaimed as we

watched her belly flop into a drift. "That was some wipeout."

He and I did sharp hockey stops, sending snow flying. "Lily, are you all right?" I asked, sidestepping over to her. She didn't answer right away, and suddenly I felt a stab of fear. God, maybe she's hurt, I thought, or . . . "Lily!" I cried, my voice shrill with fear.

Lily sat up groggily. Relief flooded through me. "I . . . got . . . the . . . wind . . . knocked . . . out . . . of . . . me," she panted, flopping onto her back with her arms flung out. "Ugh."

When Lily had caught her breath, Jack helped her to her feet. She was still wobbly, so he kept his arm around her waist.

"Are you going to be okay?" I asked her. Lily nodded, but she didn't look as if she meant it. "Maybe you should sit back down," I suggested, steadying her with a gloved hand.

"I'll just take it slow," she said.

That was an understatement. Lily was so shaky, Jack had to practically carry her down the slope. Now that I was over my worry, I started to get annoyed with her again. It was truly amazing how she always managed to wedge herself into the center of every situation.

I studied the pair of them, thinking that Jack might be losing his patience with Lily, too, but his expression was good-humored. He was being a sport about the whole thing.

That's when I noticed the look on my sister's

face. I blinked, wondering if I'd imagined it, but
Lily was still gazing at Jack with adoration in her
blue eyes. She'd be drooling soon if she didn't
watch it. Lily has a crush on Jack! I realized.

I tried to remember if I'd ever seen her act
moony around him before, but I didn't come up
with much. Maybe she'd had a crush on him forever. And why shouldn't she? He was a cute
older guy who'd always been nice to her in a big-
brotherly way.

We got to the bottom of the hill without anyone falling down again. Jack was talking about
where to stop for a burger on the way home,
oblivious. Lily went to return her snowboard
and I watched her go, my feelings muddled. My
sister has a crush on my boyfriend, I thought. I
decided this was harmless—I knew how much
Jack cared for me; Lily couldn't really be a
threat. It made me think, though. I glanced
sideways at Jack as we carried our skis and poles
to his car and pictured Lily's worshipful look.
Do my eyes ever glow like that when *I* look at
him? I wondered.

Somehow I doubted it.

"It didn't really work," I reported to Ellen the
next day. Her parents were out, and I was helping
her keep an eye on her kid brothers.

As Caleb and Quinn ran around the house in
Superman capes, trying to karate chop each other,
I told Ellen the abridged version of our trip to

Cabot Mountain. She laughed. "Maybe you should stick to quiet walks in the woods."

"Maybe," I said.

"I wouldn't worry. You two are a great couple. Hey, Quinn! Caleb! Cut it out!"

We managed to keep the boys from tearing the house apart until Mr. and Mrs. Adams got back. Late in the afternoon I walked home. For no particular reason I took a roundabout route, following a back road that rolls up and down hills with an occasional view of the ocean. I wanted to be alone with my thoughts.

Not that my thoughts were so comforting. I was still wondering what I should do about Jack. Ellen said we were a great couple. Were we, really? What did that even mean?

I needed advice, and I knew who I wanted to ask. There was one person I'd always been able to go to when I had something on my mind. One person who never laughed at my questions. One person I trusted to be understanding and kind.

The road curved, and I found myself at the back of the little white church that my family attended. Beyond it was the cemetery.

I cut over to the gate and paused. I could see Daisy's and Dad's headstones. The wreaths Lily had brought back in December were gone—I guessed the groundskeeper had eventually removed them.

If it works for Lily, I decided, pushing open the gate, maybe it will work for me.

I sat down on the cold, hard ground near Daisy's grave. For a minute I didn't speak. Even though the cemetery was deserted, so no one could see me, it seemed too silly. I ventured a single word. "Hi," I whispered.

The wind made the bare tree branches murmur.

I tried again. "I have a boyfriend, Daze," I told her. "Isn't that a riot? It's Jack. That would have made you happy, wouldn't it? You always liked him. Everybody does. He's like a son to Mom and a brother to Rose and Lily. He belongs with us. But . . ."

I stopped, hunching my neck down into the collar of my coat. A chipmunk scurried between two nearby headstones. "But it doesn't feel right, Daze. Something's missing. I don't know what it is." I paused again, searching my heart for the response Daisy might have given if she were alive. "Talk to him, right? I know I should, but I'm scared. What if he gets mad? I can't risk that."

I waited to feel Daisy's presence, but I didn't. Not really.

I sighed. "I wish I could talk to you, Daisy," I said sadly. "I could talk to Rose, I guess. She's always been a good big sister to me. But we're just not as close as you and I were. Besides, she's so busy with all of that wedding stuff. Mom? She's working constantly. We never have time to talk. Lily? I don't think so."

I got to my feet and stared at Daisy's gravestone, reading her name and the dates over and over. My eyes blurred with tears. "I miss you so much, Daze," I whispered. "I thought it would get better with time, but it doesn't. It gets worse."

When I'd cried my fill for now, I walked slowly out of the cemetery. Back on the road, it was only a quarter of a mile to Main Street. I was home. But home seemed as cold and hopeless as the graveyard. I still had questions and no answers.

Ten

"I look like a sofa," I declared, twisting to see my back in the mirror at the bridal shop in the mall.

Lily's voice floated over the wall between the dressing rooms. "It looks good on me."

Rose was standing outside. "Do you really think it makes you look big, Toad?" she asked. "Come out here so I can see."

Lily and I emerged from our dressing rooms. Rose inspected the bridesmaid dresses we were wearing, tugging at the necklines, adjusting the sleeves, and retying the bows at our waists. "A sofa?" she said to me.

"It's just so . . . floral," I explained. "Weren't there some plain navy blue dresses on the rack?"

"I *like* flowers, though," Rose said.

"And it's Rose's wedding," Lily piped up. "She's the bride."

Rose handed me three more flowered dresses to try on. I shuffled back into the dressing room with a sigh. "Right. It's Rose's wedding."

It was Rose's wedding, but somehow it seemed to have spiraled out of control—to me, at least. It had taken over the world, or our household, anyway. Whenever Rose came home lately, all anyone talked about was the wedding: flowers and cakes, dresses and honeymoons, guest lists and gift registries. Cath and Rox would come over to rehearse the songs they were going to sing during the ceremony and giggle about the nightgown Rose had bought for her wedding night. It never ended.

When I'd tried on six dresses, I stomped out of the dressing room in my underwear, not caring who saw me. "Can you just pick something?" I begged Rose. "We've been here all morning!"

Rose frowned as she pushed me back into the dressing room. Following me in, she yanked the curtain closed behind us. "This is important, Laurel. You can't wear your overalls, you know."

"No one's going to be looking at the bridesmaids. You're the main attraction," I pointed out as I pulled on my overalls and turtleneck. "Does it really matter what we wear?"

"Of course!" Rose clearly couldn't believe my ignorance. "Do you want me to gag every time I look at my wedding photos?"

I supposed that *would* be pretty bad. "I still think you should make up your mind. I want to get to the WRC before the sun sets."

Rose gathered up the discarded bridesmaid's dresses, acting offended. "Well, sorry I've been wasting your valuable time. I didn't realize it would kill you to show a little interest in something that means so much to me."

Immediately I felt like a jerk. "I'm sorry, Rose," I said contritely. "I *do* care about the dresses. I like . . . that one." I pointed to a dress at random.

"Really?" Rose perked up. "That's the one I was leaning toward, too."

"Me too," Lily said.

"Then let's do it," Rose declared.

The saleswoman recorded our measurements and Rose ordered the dresses, which were going to be a gift from Stephen's mother. Then we headed out into the mall. "Come with me to look at wedding rings," Rose said.

The three of us went into a jewelry store. I didn't want to hurt Rose's feelings again, so I pretended to be fascinated by the different cuts and carats and what have you.

"So, Toad," Rose said. "I've cleared a weekend in May for the bridal shower. Have you thought about where you want to have it?"

"No," I admitted. "Where do *you* want to have it?"

"You could do it at a restaurant or at home," Rose replied. "I'm sure the Applebys or the Beales would be happy to host it, too."

"So, there's a meal involved?"

"If you want. It's up to you, Toad. You're the maid of honor."

The maid of honor. I felt paralyzed. "Um . . . I'll let you know what I decide, okay?"

"Okay." Rose pointed at a gold wedding band. "What do you think about this one, Lil? Too plain?"

Lily gushed over the ring's simplicity and elegance. I felt ill. I'd been hoping I'd be able to find a way to get out of arranging the shower, but that was starting to look impossible.

I spent the afternoon at the WRC, helping Carlos and Griffin lead a workshop for new volunteers, one of whom was Jon Rotner. When I came home for dinner, Rose met me at the door. "You're just in time," she announced. "Come on."

I followed her and Mom upstairs. On our way we grabbed Lily from in front of the computer. "You're on that machine night and day," Mom said.

Lily shrugged. "What are we doing?" she asked.

"Looking for Mom's wedding dress," Rose explained.

There was a small attic over our apartment that was crammed with all the stuff that used to be in our much bigger attic in the house on Lighthouse Road. When we'd all crowded up there, Mom contemplated a couple of old cedar chests. "It's in one of these," she said. "Here, help me open them."

Mom and I lifted the lid on the first chest while Rose and Lily opened the other. "It's not in here," Lily said, "but check out these cool shoes! Were they yours, Mom? Can I have them?"

She held up a pair of platforms. Mom laughed. "In a million years I would never have guessed that those would come back into fashion. Sure, you can have them. Just be careful not to fall off them and break your neck."

Inside the chest Mom and I had opened was a large, flat cardboard box. "This must be the dress," I said, opening the box.

Ivory satin peeked through layers of ancient tissue paper. "Look, it hasn't yellowed at all," Rose exclaimed. "It's still as white as snow."

As Mom carefully lifted the dress from the box my sisters oohed and aahed. Even I caught my breath. We'd all seen pictures of Mom in her dress, but it was even more glamorous in real life, with off-the-shoulder sleeves and a fitted bodice flaring out to a full skirt with a long train. "It's beautiful," Lily gushed. "Look at that tiny waist."

Mom held the dress against her body, a wistful smile on her face. "I was a size six back then."

"You're so slim—you could still fit in it," I said.

"What was *your* wedding day like, Mom?" Rose asked.

"It was June, like yours will be, Rose. A beautiful day. I had four bridesmaids, just like you, in shell pink dresses. We all wore traditional clothing—your father looked very handsome in his morning suit. But the actual ceremony was a little unconventional. The minister married us on the deck of your father's fishing boat."

"You're kidding!" Rose said. "Why didn't we know that?"

"Maybe because we had the formal portraits taken on my parents' porch," Mom replied, "and because no one ever asked me."

She held out the dress to Rose. Talking about

her wedding to Dad had brought tears to her eyes. "What do you think? Too old-fashioned?"

"No, it's perfect," Rose said. "I want to wear it, Mom. Is that okay?"

"Of course it's okay." Mom hugged Rose. "Nothing would make me happier."

Now Rose started to cry, too. "What is it, honey?" Mom asked.

"I wish Daisy were here," Rose answered, sniffling. She turned to me. "That doesn't mean I don't love you, too, Toad. I'm glad you're going to be my maid of honor. But she should be here to share my wedding day with me." I nodded to show I understood. Rose didn't really need to explain it to me—I felt the same way she did. "And so should Daddy," she added in a whisper.

Mom nodded.

Everyone was quiet for a moment, and suddenly the attic felt full of ghosts. "Let's go back downstairs," I suggested quietly.

We took turns climbing down the pull-down ladder.

In my room Rose laid the dress on the bed she sleeps in when she's home. "Maybe *you'll* wear this someday, Toad," she said.

"Yeah, right," I said, still looking at the dress.

Lily, Rose, and Mom headed downstairs to start dinner. I lingered in my room for a minute. I couldn't take my eyes off the layers of white satin. I should put it in the closet, I thought. So Snickers won't get her paws on it.

I picked up the dress. The yards and yards of fabric made it heavy, and the satin was incredibly smooth. Walking across the room, I stopped halfway, Rose's words in my head. "Maybe you'll wear this someday. . . ."

I lifted up the dress, holding it against my body, and looked at myself in the mirror over my dresser. Would I ever get married? Probably not, I decided. A wildlife biologist who spent months at a time in the field wouldn't exactly have time for a husband and kids. But the dress *was* pretty. . . .

Still looking in the mirror, I tried to picture myself as a bride, wearing Mom's gown and holding a bouquet of wildflowers picked in Meredith's Meadow. I supposed I'd need a groom. Jack? My eyes grew dreamy. I had a sudden vision of myself standing at the altar, but who was that? Facing me with my hand in his and slipping a gold ring on my finger was . . . Carlos Alvarez.

Carlos? I blinked in surprise and the vision faded. Confused, I shoved the wedding dress onto a hanger in the closet and slammed the door fast.

Jack and I had a date that night. We went to a party at Eric's and then parked at the beach to look at the stars. Even though my fantasy about marrying Carlos had been totally unintentional, not to mention ridiculous, and even though of course there was no way Jack could ever find out about it, in fact no one on the *planet* would ever know, I still felt guilty, so I tried as hard as I could to make it a romantic evening. We had a major make-out session in Jack's car. When we finally said good night, he had kind of a dazed, happy look on his face. "See you at school on Monday," he murmured, giving my neck one last nuzzle.

"Um-hm," I said.

"I love you so much, it hurts."

I never know how to respond when he says stuff like that, so I settled for, "Same here."

He walked me up to the door of the apartment. We kissed for a few more minutes. "This feels so good. Do we really have to stop?" he asked.

"I need to get to bed," I told him. I yawned, just to prove it was true.

"I wish I could come with you."

"Sorry." I laughed.

We kissed one last time, and then Jack headed reluctantly back down the stairs to the street. Inside the apartment, I went quietly to my room. Rose had fallen asleep with the light on, a copy of *Modern Bride* magazine on the bed beside her.

As I turned out the light I heard something clatter against the glass of the window. I crossed the room and looked down. Jack was standing on the sidewalk, about to toss another pebble.

I opened the window and leaned out. "What are you doing?"

"I just wanted to tell you that you mean the world to me."

What was I supposed to say to that? Sometimes

Jack is a little overboard with his feelings. I ended up just saying, "Good."

We blew some kisses, and then I closed the window. Amazingly, considering all the noise, Rose hadn't woken up. Putting on some pajamas, I climbed into my bed.

For a long time I lay with my head on the pillow, staring into the darkness. I still couldn't quite believe that I had a boyfriend who threw pebbles at my window to tell me he was crazy about me. Something bothered me, though. Whenever Jack said something like, "You mean the world to me," I could never say it back. The words stuck in my throat.

I'm just not the demonstrative type, I decided. But was that it, really? I thought back on the evening, particularly parking at the beach. I couldn't lie to myself. No matter how warm the kisses, I'd still felt cool inside.

I rolled over, my face to the wall. I'll talk to him about it soon, I decided, then started thinking about Rose's bridal shower. I finally fell asleep and dreamed about stones hitting my windowpane and cemeteries and baby seals in shell pink dresses.

Eleven

"Wow. Feel that wind," Ellen said.

Jack pointed to the sky. "Check out the clouds."

"A nor'easter," Eric said.

It was late Friday afternoon and a bunch of us were leaving the school building, on our way to Cap'n Jack's for burgers. The wind whipped my long hair out behind me. I shivered, and not just from the cold. A storm was definitely brewing, and weather like this always reminded me of the storm that swamped my father's fishing boat.

At Cap'n Jack's six of us squeezed into a booth: me, Jack, Ellen, Eric, Monica, and Nikolai, another buddy of Jack's. We'd gone to an after-school college fair, so naturally that was what we talked about.

"Look at all this stuff." Monica dumped the contents of her backpack on the table. About a hundred college brochures spilled out. "How are we ever supposed to decide?"

Our waitress had just delivered a big basket of french fries, and Eric reached for one. "You narrow it down," he said. "You know, big public university or small private college? What kind of major do you want, hard science or liberal arts? Stay in New England or move someplace else?"

"I really like Stanford." Nikolai picked up a brochure and held it up so we could all see the palm trees. "Palo Alto, California. It looks warm."

Monica laughed. "That's your reason?"

Nikolai grinned. "It's as good as any."

"I don't want to go that far away," Ellen remarked, pouring some soda from the pitcher into her glass.

"I go back and forth," I said, dipping a french fry into the ketchup. "Sometimes I want to stay close to home, like maybe Colby or Bates. Then I think, what about the University of Virginia or Berkeley or Northwestern?"

"I thought we were going to apply to Williams and Amherst," Jack said to me.

"I know those are your favorites," I replied, "but bigger schools have more science classes to choose from."

"But we have to go to the same place." Jack slipped an arm around my shoulders and gave me a possessive squeeze. "I would miss you too much if we were apart. Besides, a long-distance relationship is a hassle, you know?"

I started to say that in my opinion, relationships in general were a hassle, but I bit my tongue. Why do we have to do everything together? I wondered. It was the science fair all over again.

Ellen was sitting across from me, and she

caught my eye. My feelings must have shown on my face because she gave me a small, sympathetic smile. I shrugged. "It's too soon to make up our minds, anyway," I concluded. "We aren't seniors yet."

We finished our burgers and headed back outside. The days were getting longer—the sun wouldn't set for another hour or so—but it was almost as dark as night. As we walked across the parking lot raindrops began to fall. Within seconds it was a downpour. "Another thing about Stanford," Nikolai shouted as we sprinted to the cars. "It hardly ever rains!"

Jack walked me to the door, holding an umbrella over my head. "See you in about an hour," he said.

We were going dancing later at the Rusty Nail—I just needed to change my clothes. I don't really like to dance, but it's the most popular place for South Regional couples to hang out, so Jack and I went there pretty often. "See you," I echoed.

Bending, Jack brushed the corner of my mouth with a kiss. While he hurried back to his car in the rain, I ducked into the building.

Inside, I found a note from Mom on the kitchen counter: *I'm working until ten or so. Chicken pie in the fridge—heat at 350 and make a salad.*

I preheated the oven, then headed upstairs. As I passed the family room I saw Lily at the computer. I almost walked past, but then I stopped and went into the room, curious. "Surfing the net again?" I asked.

At the sound of my voice, she jumped a little. I stepped closer, and she quickly hit a few keys in a secretive, I-don't-want-you-to-see-what-I'm-doing way.

"Chat room?" I guessed.

Lily swiveled in her chair. Her cheeks were pink. "Do you really care?" she challenged.

I did, a little. Lately no one had time to monitor Lily's computer use. But I didn't have time to get into some intense discussion with my sister. "I'm just changing, then I'm going out with Jack, so you're on your own for dinner," I told her. "I'll put the chicken pie in the oven and set the timer. Listen for the buzzer, okay?"

Lily's expression grew even more sulky. "Fine," she said as she turned back to the computer.

I went upstairs, wondering about Lily and the Internet. Poetry? Boys? A cult? I didn't dwell on it for long, though—I was too busy staring into my closet. I hated dressing up, but I had one skirt and a chenille top that Jack really liked. Instead I reached for a clean pair of overalls folded on the shelf. I wasn't sure why, but tonight I didn't feel like dressing to make my boyfriend happy.

As I turned back around, a gust of wind rattled the windowpanes. I looked out into the grayness. Rain was falling in sheets and lightning flickered in the distance. A few seconds later thunder rumbled.

Again I shivered. It's not a good night to go out, I thought. I remembered waving to Daisy as she drove off into the rain the day after my birthday. Storms never brought good things to my family. What did this one hold in store?

The phone rang at seven o'clock the next morning. I sat up in bed, my heart pounding. *Daisy*, I thought, reliving that phone call in the middle of the night. But of course the call couldn't be about Daisy. Not anymore.

I ran out to grab the phone on the hall table, hoping it wouldn't wake up Mom. She'd been up late the night before, balancing the books for her catering business after getting home from a job. "Hello?" I said, my voice scratchy with sleep.

"Laurel?" a male voice asked.

"Speaking."

"It's Carlos."

"Carlos, hi," I said. "Why are *you* calling at the crack of dawn?"

"I'm at the center," he answered. "I came early on a hunch, and I was right. All this rain—the creek is over its banks. And it's still coming down. Another hour and it'll be flooding the paddocks and hutches. Griffin's in DC at a conference. Can you get over here and help?"

"I'll be there in ten minutes."

"I knew I could count on you."

I scribbled a note for Mom quickly, dressed quickly, and drove quickly. About a mile out of town the Old Boston Post Road dipped to pass under a bridge. The low part of the road was flooded. Keeping my fingers crossed, I plowed through, water splashing up over the hubcaps. Nothing happened—the engine didn't stall—and I made it to the WRC in ten minutes, just as I'd promised.

But ten minutes turned out to be long enough to start having doubts. Why did Carlos call me? I wondered. I wasn't as physically strong as some of the volunteers, like Jon. What if animals drowned because I didn't work fast enough? It would be all my fault.

Throwing on my slicker as I went, I hurried around to the back of the building. Just as Carlos had said, Goose Creek had swollen into a raging river. Water was already rushing under the fences of the far paddocks, and I spotted Carlos leading a skittish yearling fawn by a halter. I ran over to him. He glanced at me briskly, his dark hair wet from the rain. "Good, you're here."

"Is Lefty all right?" I asked.

Carlos nodded. "The building's high enough. Come on."

In the urgency of the moment, my fears evaporated. Carlos and I worked together for an hour moving animals—deer, bear cubs, a coyote, an injured moose, raccoons—into the building or to higher ground. For the most part, we didn't speak. I knew what Carlos wanted me to do. It was as if there were a connection from his brain directly to mine—we didn't need words.

When we got the last animal to safety—a skunk—Carlos gave me a rain-soaked hug. "We did it," he declared.

My heart swelled with joy and relief and even a little pride. "We did it," I echoed.

We were still standing in the rain. Carlos hadn't been wearing a raincoat, and my hood had fallen back, so I was almost as drenched as he was. "Thanks, Laurel. You were great. No one knows the animals like you do."

I blinked away the raindrops, staring at him, and that was when it hit me. Rather, a couple of things hit me. One was that Carlos was right—I *had* been great. I'd totally kept my cool. I never would have thought I could handle something so difficult.

The other thing that hit me was that I was looking at Carlos in the same way I'd caught Lily looking at Jack that day on the ski slopes. Oh, my God, I realized. I'm in love with him.

"I think I'll head inside and—is there anything else you want me to—maybe I could . . ." I stammered.

"Go on in and get dry," Carlos recommended.

I turned away, hoping he hadn't noticed my sudden blush. Despite the rain, I felt hot. Let's see, I found myself thinking. If I'm a high school junior and he's a college sophomore, that means he's three years older than I am. Nineteen. That's not too old, is it?

Inside the building, I stripped off my raincoat

and threw it over the back of a chair. I put my hands to my cheeks—my face was still burning. I have a crush on Carlos, I thought dizzily.

It was crazy. He was older than me, and he'd never given the least indication that he thought of me as anything other than a friend. Still . . . three years wasn't *that* huge an age difference. There were plenty of girls at South Regional who dated older boys, college boys.

The age difference wasn't the real issue, though. I already *had* a boyfriend.

I bit my lip, thinking guiltily about Jack. Daydreaming about another guy isn't cheating, I told myself. But I couldn't ignore what was happening. The charge of intense physical attraction I'd felt for Carlos was nothing like the warm, fuzzy feelings I had for Jack. I've never felt that way about Jack, I thought, and I never will.

The rain had let up by the time I met Jack after work that afternoon. I had tried to push my thoughts about Carlos out of my mind, but it was difficult. As we walked along Main Street, trying to decide where to go for a bite to eat, I told him about saving the animals at the WRC. "I think it was the most important thing I've ever done," I said.

"I bet," Jack replied, but he didn't really sound interested. He didn't seem to understand what a revelation it had been for me to discover that I could rise to the occasion and be utterly competent.

"Anyway," I told him, "I had this idea on my way home. About Rose's bridal shower. I've been stressing about getting everything just right. But I'm just not a conventional maid of honor, so why should the shower be conventional? My parents got married on a fishing boat—that was totally unique. What if I held the shower at the picnic tables by the creek behind the WRC?"

Jack cocked one eyebrow. "Different," he conceded.

My doubts returned instantly. "It's too weird, isn't it? Rose would hate it."

"I didn't say that. Do whatever you want to do." He gave me a teasing look. "By the way, does all this wedding talk give you any ideas?"

I stopped in my tracks. Wedding? Jack wasn't seriously thinking along those lines, was he? Then again, the way he talked about his feelings for me, it was possible. I couldn't stand it one minute longer—I couldn't keep pretending I felt something I didn't. I couldn't mislead him anymore. It would only be worse in the end for him if I didn't say something now. "Jack, I can't do this," I told him.

He looked at me, his forehead creased. "If you're not hungry, we don't have to—"

I shook my head. "No. I can't do *this*."

I took my hand away from his. We stood on the sidewalk, facing each other. Jack still looked puzzled, and I wished more than anything that I'd kept my mouth shut, but it was too late. The air was still wet with rain, reminding me of Carlos at the WRC that morning. I had to finish what I'd started.

"What are you talking about?" Jack asked.

I took a deep breath. "I'm talking about our relationship."

"What about it?"

"I—I don't think we should go out anymore."

He stared at me, his eyes wide with shock and disbelief. "Why? What's wrong?"

"It's not that I don't love you," I said quickly. "I do. You're my best friend. But I . . . I don't love you the way you want me to love you."

Now his expression turned stony. "What's been going on, then? Are you saying that for months you've been—"

"Maybe I should've figured this out sooner," I cut in. "But it's confusing because I do love you. I'm just not *in* love with you. I never, ever meant to do anything to hurt you. You've helped me so much, but going on like this wouldn't be fair to either of us."

"I still don't get it." Jack stuck his hands deep in the pockets of his coat. "Haven't I treated you okay?" He smiled crookedly. "I can change—just tell me what you're looking for. Different hair, different clothes, different friends . . ."

"Jack, it's not about *hair.*" I lifted my hands to my face, covering my eyes. I couldn't stand seeing the pain behind his smile. "You're a great person. I don't want you to change. But—"

"But you're dumping me."

The seconds passed. I had to look at him.

My hands dropped, and I met his eyes. They were glittering with tears. "It's not dumping. It's—"

"And right in the middle of Main Street." His voice cracked. "Gee, thanks, Laurel."

Jack turned. I grabbed his arm. "Wait," I pleaded. "Can't we talk about this some more? I want us to stay friends, to go back to the way we were before we became a couple and stopped being our real selves."

"This *is* my real self, Laurel!" he said hoarsely. "What do you think I am? A machine? You can punch a button and we shift back to being platonic, like all these months meant nothing?"

"I still want to spend time with you, though. I still want—"

"It won't work. It's got to be all or nothing." Jack clenched his jaw; I could tell he was trying not to cry. "Because you might not be in love with me, Laurel, but I'm in love with you."

I couldn't think of anything else to say. Jack gave me one last look and then he turned away, and this time I let him go.

I watched him stride off down the sidewalk, and now I was crying, too. An elderly woman coming out of the Down East News and Drugstore saw the tears on my face. "Are you all right, dear?" she asked.

I nodded. "I'm all right."

I wasn't, though. Not at all.

Twelve

"**B**oy, are you stupid."

That was Lily's comment that night after she overheard me telling Mom that I'd broken up with Jack.

We were in the upstairs hallway. "Shut up, okay?" I snapped, stomping to my room. "I never asked for your opinion."

I slammed the door, but not before she could yell after me, "He was too good for you, anyway!"

The rest of the weekend was dismal. I moped around, too depressed even to play with Snickers or Alfalfa. When Monday morning dawned, I looked unhappily out my window. The sky was blue, trees were budding, birds were singing, but it didn't mean anything to me. My canoe and paddles were practically crying out to hit the water again after a long winter in the storage room behind Wissinger's Bakery. Meredith's Meadow would be a rainbow of wildflowers. It didn't matter. For the first time in my life, I didn't want to leave the house. Most of all, I dreaded school.

I considered pretending to be sick, but I knew Mom would see right through me. Maybe Jack will stay home, I thought as I rode the school bus. If I was feeling rotten, he had to be feeling worse.

I ran into him right off the bat, naturally. We were heading in opposite directions in the main hall at South Regional, both walking to our lockers. I started to say hi, but he kept looking straight ahead, not even acknowledging me, so I swallowed the greeting.

Word gets around school fast when a couple gets together or breaks up, but not everyone had heard by lunchtime. I was sitting with Ellen when Jack walked across the cafeteria with a couple of guys from his wrestling team. None of them was his close friend—they weren't people Jack would have told about our breakup. "Should we sit there?" asked one of the guys, Luis, nodding toward my table.

Without speaking, Jack steered Luis in another direction, his face a blank mask.

"I hate this," I whispered, staring down at my sandwich. I couldn't eat a bite.

Ellen patted my hand, then offered me an Oreo. I gazed after Jack, my heart aching. Did I do the right thing? I wondered.

There was a science club meeting after school. It was one place I knew I'd be safe from bumping into Jack—even though he'd wanted to do the science fair project with me, he'd never really been into that sort of stuff.

"Speaking of which," I said to Ellen with a

heavy sigh. We'd taken seats in the back of the room. "Jack and I didn't get that far on our project. There's no way I can finish it on my own in just one week."

"Tell you what." Ellen took a spiral notebook out of her backpack and opened it up. "I still have a lot to do myself." She pushed her glasses up on her freckled nose, then pointed to a page. "Three experiments. Why don't you help me?"

I looked at Ellen. "That's really nice of you."

The senior who's president of the club, Mimi Grange, called the meeting to order. The club started to discuss plans for setting up the science fair the following week.

Ellen handed me her notebook so I could read the notes she'd written on her experiments so far. We're both into environmental stuff, and her project was about how natural things like algae could purify contaminated water. I found myself nodding as I read along—she'd designed some good experiments.

I nudged her with my elbow. "Did you think about trying it on salt water, too?" I whispered.

"Salinity kills the algae," she whispered back.

"But what if you . . ."

We whispered back and forth until Mimi gave us a dirty look. Then I switched to scribbling notes. Twenty minutes later I realized that I'd temporarily forgotten how horrible everything was with Jack. My heart was still sore from losing Daisy, and now another important person had been torn from my life, in a different way, but still. It was my choice this time, I reminded myself; I did the right thing. And maybe there *was* life after breaking up.

I came home to a quiet house. As usual Mom had left a note on the kitchen counter: *I'm at a meeting in Portland. Be back around eight.*

I sighed deeply. I don't have a mother lately, I thought, just a pile of paper scraps. Immediately I felt bad for being so selfish. Mom was doing her best. She worked hard for all of us, not just for herself. But I'd rather have less money and see her more often, I decided.

I left the note out in case Lily hadn't seen it yet, although I assumed she was already home from school—she doesn't have extracurricular activities on Monday. Mom's note hadn't mentioned supper. "Lily?" I called, walking out into the hall. "Want to order a pizza?"

The only answer was silence. "Lily," I yelled again. I glanced into the family room. The computer was on, but Lily was nowhere in sight. I walked over. Lily was always extremely secretive about her computer habits, but for once she'd left her e-mail folder open. I couldn't resist—leaning close to the bright screen, I read the most recent message.

It was kind of shocking. *Dear Tigerlilli*, her correspondent wrote. *I could tell from your last letter that you're really sad. Your family sounds like they don't understand you at all. Why don't you just get out of there? You know you want to. I have plenty of room at my place. A double bed. :-) Write back and tell me where to meet you. XXOO, J.H.*

I whirled on my heel. "Lily!" I shouted. My gaze fell on the coffee table. Running over, I seized a brochure. "The bus schedule," I said aloud, suddenly in a panic. "Oh, my God, she ran away."

I sprinted out of the room . . . and barreled straight into Lily. We both screamed. "What's wrong?" she asked. "I thought I heard you yelling—I was in the bathroom."

"What's *wrong?*" I gasped, pointing to the computer. "That's what's wrong!"

Lily hurried over to the computer and closed her e-mail file. "You shouldn't have been reading my private stuff," she exclaimed angrily.

"Lily, what's going on?"

She turned to face me, her arms folded tightly across her chest. "Nothing."

"Come on," I pressed. "Are you thinking of running away with whoever that is? J.H.? Who is he, anyway?"

"What difference would it make to you?" she retorted. "People on the Internet care more about me than you do!"

I stared at my sister. She'd turned fourteen over the winter, and she was starting to fill out. She had a curvier figure than me now, and in some of her getups—like today's psychedelic seventies micromini—she looked precociously grown-up. I could still see the little girl under the surface, though. A little girl who needed a big sister. And with Daisy gone and Rose in college, that leaves me, I realized with a pang as I remembered all the times in the past few months that Lily had tried to get my attention and I'd told her to get lost. What had I been thinking? I couldn't stand to lose another sister.

"Lily, I'm sorry," I said. "I've been so caught up in my own life lately, I haven't kept track of what's going on with you."

Lily narrowed her eyes at me. *"Lately?* How about *forever.*"

"Tell me about J.H.," I said.

Lily rolled her eyes. "We met in this chat room," she explained, "and at first I thought he was really interesting. It was his initials, partly." She blushed slightly. "I knew he wasn't Jack Harrison, obviously, but I thought maybe he was as nice as Jack."

"But that line about his double bed—"

"Can you believe that?" Lily exclaimed. "What a creep! Like I would really run off with some guy I'd never even met in person! I'm glad I didn't tell him my real name."

I was so relieved, I rushed over and gave her a hug. "Oh, Lily. You're crazy. You know that?"

"Not as crazy as you." She pushed me away. "I still can't believe you broke up with the coolest, sweetest guy in Maine."

"Here's the thing," I said, figuring I might as well confide in Lily as anyone. "He *is* the coolest, sweetest guy in Maine. But I just didn't feel . . ." I thought about the jolt I'd gotten from Carlos the other day in the rain. "Sparks."

"I don't know." Lily shook her head. "Sparks might not be all they're cracked up to be. Like, Tom Muldoone? This guy in my math class? Talk about sparks. But I happen to know he's a real jerk to the girls he goes out with. I wouldn't want to date him. I think it would be the ultimate to go out with a guy who was my best friend, like you and Jack, or Rose and Stephen."

"I thought so too at first." I sighed. "But it just wasn't right."

"I guess he'll have to wait for me to grow up, then," said Lily, smiling mischievously.

I thought about the age difference between me and Carlos. Lily and Jack? It wasn't impossible. "Maybe," I agreed, smiling back at her.

Lily and I ended up curled up on the couch, talking about boys. We had a pizza delivered and ate the whole thing, still talking. It was as if some wall that had stood between us for years and years had tumbled. Then again, maybe the wall wasn't gone altogether—we still disagreed about nearly everything—but it had some major cracks in it. It was almost like the old days, gabbing with Daisy.

When the pizza was gone and we'd polished off a pint of ice cream, too, I asked Lily, "What are you going to do about J.H.? The e-mail guy?"

"Write back and tell him I was *about* to run off with him, but my big sister wouldn't let me," she answered, her eyes twinkling, "so I decided to save myself for Mr. Right."

"I guess I'll do the same," I said.

The science fair is a pretty big deal. The kids who win prizes always get into really good colleges and win scholarships and things like that. A week later, on Monday night Ellen and I had a display table near the door to the gym—there were students from three regional high schools competing—so the judges looked at our project first, but that didn't end up helping. They took some notes and moved on to the next exhibit pretty quickly. "Not a good sign," Ellen said with a sigh.

While we waited for the judging, we took turns wandering around the gym, looking at other people's projects and getting sodas at the concession table. I stopped to talk to Jon about his homemade telescope. "You're going to win," I predicted. He'd set up a really ingenious experiment to track comets.

"I'm not so sure," Jon replied. "Did you see the girls from Kent with the solar-powered robot?"

I walked over to look at the robot. A lot of kids from South Regional were at the fair to see how their friends did and just to check out the cool exhibits. I couldn't believe it when I saw Jack walking my way.

He must have come here to see me! I thought,

my heart pounding. He changed his mind—he wants to stay friends after all. "Jack," I called.

He must have heard me—we weren't *that* far apart—but instead of continuing toward me, he pivoted and headed in a different direction. "Hey," I heard him say to someone. "How's it going?"

My cheeks crimson, I hurried back to my booth, hoping no one had witnessed me getting totally iced by my ex. A few minutes ago I'd been feeling pretty good. My life seemed to be getting back to normal. But Jack blowing me off like that was like a knife twisting in my heart. Without his friendship, there was an empty place in my life that I didn't think would ever be filled.

Jon won a prize, but Ellen and I didn't, not even honorable mention. Ellen was disappointed, but I wasn't really surprised. You don't win if you don't give something one hundred percent. That was what Daisy always said, and that was how she'd lived her life.

I was starting to believe I'd never win at anything.

Thirteen

Rose came home one weekend in early May for her long-awaited bridal shower. I'd arranged with Griffin to use the WRC on a Sunday, when it's usually closed.

Lily and I went over early to decorate the picnic tables by the creek with tablecloths and balloon bouquets. "The weather's great," she observed. "That's lucky."

"Yeah," I agreed, glancing upward. The sky was blue, so it looked like I didn't have to worry about rain, but I was nervous about everything else. "What if she doesn't like it, though?"

"She's going to get tons of presents," Lily replied. "What's not to like?"

I still wasn't sure about my choice, but it was too late to back out now. I'd gone with my gut and decided to make the bridal shower nontraditional, like me. There wouldn't be any china or silver. We were going to have bagels and cream cheese and fruit salad on paper plates, with deer and raccoons and a fox and a moose watching us from the other side of the lawn.

I was excited in spite of myself. I wanted Rose to like the shower so badly!

"Let's head back to the apartment," I said to Lily. "I've made the dough, but I still need to bake the cookies."

Back at the apartment, I was a nervous wreck. I kept trying—and failing—to do a hundred things at once. I thought I'd have enough time to fix my hair while the cookies were baking, but the smell of something burning as I was tying up my braid proved me wrong. I ran down the stairs to find Lily pulling the cookies out of the oven—and blowing the smoke off them.

"They aren't badly burned," she told me.

"Well," I said, eyeing my singed desserts, "they'll have to do. I don't have time to make more."

At ten-thirty I was back at the Wildlife Rescue Center—the bridal shower guests started arriving at eleven. I'd invited Mom and Lily, of course, and Rose's high school friends Cath and Rox and their mothers. Mita was there, although *her* mother lived in Boston now and couldn't make it because she had to work at her Indian restaurant. Rose's BU roommates, Beverly and Julia, came, and Stephen's mom and sisters.

Everyone exclaimed about the WRC. "Isn't this a lovely setting?" "How unusual!" "Are those animals tame?"

I hadn't told Rose beforehand where the party was going to be, and I was chewing my nails as I waited for her reaction. To my vast relief, she gave me a big hug and said, "This is fantastic, Toad."

"It's going well, don't you think?" I whispered

to Lily a little while later. The guests were eating bagels and chatting—things seemed to be going smoothly.

"You pulled it off," Lily whispered back.

That's when the guests discovered the cookies.

"Oooh—chocolate chocolate chip!" Val Mathias said. "My favorite!"

I was about to warn her that they weren't double chocolate chip—they were just regular chocolate chip set on "extra crispy"—but she had already taken a big bite. So had Mita and Mrs. Mathias. I have to say that their expressions would have been hilarious if I hadn't been so embarrassed.

"Let's do the presents," I suggested as everyone grabbed napkins and tried to dispose of their cookies as discreetly as possible.

Rose smiled. "I'm ready."

There were two tall stacks of packages, all wrapped in glittery paper with lots of ribbons and bows. I handed Rose the first present . . . just as the first raindrop fell.

Hurriedly we all moved inside—but we weren't fast enough. Rose opened her gifts in the charmless lobby of the WRC while the rest of the guests tried to dry themselves off. I don't even remember what Rose got—I was only concentrating on trying not to burst into tears.

When the party was over and only Mom, Lily, Rose, and I were left, I put my hands to my face. "I can't believe I wrecked your one and only chance at a bridal shower," I groaned.

Rose looked surprised. "What are you talking about?" she asked.

"See?" I turned to my mother. "You were right not to let me help at your parties, Mom. I can't do anything right. I'm going to drop my bouquet and trip going down the aisle, Rose, I just know it. I'm such a spaz."

"Toad, I *loved* my shower," Rose said.

I rolled my eyes. "Please. You don't have to lie about it."

"Seriously," she insisted. "Maybe it wasn't perfect, but it was special! I'll never forget it."

"It was very original," Mom put in. "I'm impressed that you did it all yourself—the locale, the food, the invitations. You didn't even ask me for help!"

"I didn't want to bother you," I explained. "You're too busy as it is."

"Well, I thought it was offbeat and perfect," Rose declared, giving me a hug. "You put a lot of yourself into it, and that's what means the most to me. I only hope I have half as much fun at my wedding!"

I sighed. There was no use crying over spilled milk or soggy bagels. "Let's go home," I said.

I wouldn't let Rose clean up, so she and Lily went to look at Lefty while Mom helped me out. She and I ran out into the rain to get all the trash off the picnic tables. We carried the leftover food and supplies and Rose's gifts to the car. We didn't speak until everything was done. Then, before I could call Rose and Lily, Mom put a hand on my arm. "Laurel, sit down for a minute," she said.

We both sat down on chairs in the lobby. I looked at her apologetically. "I know the party was a mess," I began. "I should have asked you and Sarah to cater it. I really hoped that if for once I did it myself, it—"

Mom lifted a hand. "The party was fine, Laurel. Is that really what you think people think of you, though? That you can't do anything right?"

I hung my head, biting my lip.

"Laurel, I didn't want you to help with the catering because I didn't want to stress you out." She let out a sigh. "Do you remember, after Dad died, how hard we had to scramble? I leaned hard on your big sisters, especially Daisy. It was too much for her—she ended up cracking under the strain."

"You mean junior year, when she went through that rebellious stage? That wasn't your fault, Mom."

"It wasn't?" Mom shook her head. "I felt very much to blame at the time."

"Daisy just needed to let off steam," I said. "She'd always been so perfect."

"That's just it," Mom exclaimed. "I made her feel she *had* to be."

"And she was. Whereas I don't even come close, no matter how hard I try."

I hung my head again and struggled not to cry, embarrassed that Mom was witnessing me feeling so sorry for myself. When Mom put an arm around my shoulders, though, I couldn't help it. A tear trickled down my cheek.

"I think you're a very able person, Laurel May Walker," she declared.

I sniffled. "That's not how I feel."

"Laurel, you have your own special qualities and abilities." Mom gave me a squeeze. "It's true that you'll never be like Daisy, but I wouldn't want you to be. You're you, and a lot of people love you exactly as you are. Including me."

We were both thoughtful for a minute. Then Mom said, "I *am* too busy, aren't I?" I couldn't deny it. "The problem is, I've found it's the only thing that helps. If I work constantly, I don't have as much time to grieve. Do you know what I mean?"

I thought about how I'd sought refuge in my relationship with Jack. "I think so."

"It's crazy." Mom's arm tightened around me. "I've been missing one daughter so much that it's made me neglect the ones I still have. I'll make some changes, Laurel," she promised. "I'll get my work schedule under control. And if you really want to help with the business, I'd be more than glad to have you. There are a lot of things I think you could do very well."

I cracked a smile. "Like, if you need any wild animal acts."

Mom laughed. "Seriously. I don't want you not to try things just because you're afraid you might trip and fall. We all trip and fall sometimes. That doesn't mean you won't succeed sometimes, too."

"Thanks, Mom," I whispered.

She still had her arm around me. I put my head on her shoulder. "You can lean on me, too, Mom."

She tipped her head so it rested lightly on top of mine. "Okay," she said, "I will."

The rain cleared by dinnertime. After we ate, Rose went over to Rox's house, Lily sat down at the computer to write a story—she'd sworn off chat rooms for the time being—and Mom and Hal settled down to watch the news on public television. I took Snickers out for a walk.

It was seven-thirty and still light. Halfway between the spring equinox and the summer solstice, the days were getting longer and longer. I let Snickers run around in the park for a while—she was getting so big, she almost didn't look like a puppy anymore—and then walked with her through town. I was feeling better than I had in a while, thanks to my talk with Mom. Now that I looked back on it, the bridal shower hadn't been all *that* bad. Maybe I'd never be the most polished, self-confident person on the planet, but that *didn't* mean I couldn't handle things. When I forget to be afraid, I do okay, I thought, remembering the flood at the WRC.

At the end of the commercial part of Main Street, I found myself turning left on Lighthouse Road. "The sun won't set for half an hour," I told the dog. "Let's go to the beach."

With Snickers loping beside me, I followed the

road around a big curve. My family's old house stood tall behind a hedge of lilacs. The apple trees in the backyard were in bloom. Do the bluebirds still come back to the birdhouse Daisy helped me nail to the trunk of the beech tree? I wondered.

I kept walking, savoring the way the world was suddenly full of color and sound again. Frogs croaked and chuckled in the pond. Mayflies buzzed. Weeds and wildflowers were sprouting on the roadside: dandelions, chickweed, thistles, coltsfoot. The sight of them was as welcome as an old friend.

At the bottom of a long gravel driveway, I stopped. The sign hanging from the mailbox said Windy Ridge. I peered up the drive at the house on the hill, wondering. Is he home? I thought. I shouldn't show up without calling first. Not that there's any point calling—he'd refuse to talk to me.

I considered turning around. Then I chided myself for being a coward. What are you afraid of? I asked myself. You have nothing to lose.

I headed up the driveway.

"Mr. and Mrs. Harrison will flip," I warned Snickers. I hadn't seen them since Jack and I broke up, and I was sure they hated me. Snickers just tugged on the leash, wanting to chase a rabbit munching clover on the hillside.

When I got to the front door, I hesitated again. It wasn't too late to run back down the driveway. Instead I took a deep breath and rang the bell.

Jack answered the door himself. His expression wasn't exactly welcoming. "What do *you* want?"

Snickers bounced against the screen door that separated us, barking happily at the sight of Jack. "Can we talk?" I asked.

Jack shrugged. He opened the screen door, and Snickers proceeded to jump all over him. When he bent to rub her ears, she licked his face.

"I was heating up some leftover pizza," Jack said. I followed him into the kitchen. "Want a soda or something?"

"No, thanks. Are your parents around?"

Snapping open a can of root beer, he shook his head. "They drove down to Boston for the symphony."

"Oh," I said.

"What do you want, anyway?" he asked again curtly.

I looked at Jack and tried to pretend this was a normal conversation and not one of the most uncomfortable moments of my life. "I just wanted to, you know, see how you're doing. And Rose's wedding is in three weeks, and I thought maybe, well, since you're such an old friend of the family, you should really be there. I know Rose and Stephen would like that. So you should . . ." I gulped. "Come to the wedding. With me. You know, as friends."

We were standing on opposite sides of the trestle table in the Harrisons' big kitchen. "I don't think so," Jack said finally.

I gripped the back of the chair in front of me.

"Can't we get past this?" I pleaded. "I miss you. Can't we be—"

His jaw muscles tightened. "You really don't get it, do you?"

"But it's not just anybody—it's Rose and Stephen. You've known them forever and—"

"Okay, I'll spell it out for you," he interrupted me, flushing angrily. "You broke my heart, Laurel. I don't want to be around you, especially not at a wedding."

His face was red; mine turned pale. "What will it take for you to forgive me?" I whispered.

"I don't know if I ever will."

There was nothing else to say. Jack didn't walk me to the door. I let myself out, then jogged home with Snickers, trying not to cry as I hurried along Main Street. Bursting into the apartment, I almost tripped over Lily. "What's the matter?" she asked when she saw my miserable expression. "Laurel, what happened?"

Not answering her, I dropped the dog's leash and ran upstairs. Slamming the door to my room, I flung myself onto my bed. Instead of crying, though, I just lay there with my face in the pillow. I'll get over this, I told myself. I'll get over this, I'll get over this. . . .

"He's *gone?*"

I was at the Wildlife Rescue Center the following Saturday, staring into Lefty's empty pen. Carlos stood beside me. "We knew it had to hap-

pen sooner or later," he reminded me. "He'd outgrown us—he needed a real tank to swim in so he
could get ready for the ocean. Griff had the aquarium come and get him yesterday."

I turned away from the pen. "I didn't even get
to say good-bye."

"I'm sorry, Laurel. Griff and I should've called
you." Carlos rested a hand briefly on my shoulder.
On any other occasion I would have been thrilled
by this contact, but not today. I drew in a deep,
shaky breath. "It's . . . just . . . so . . . *hard.*" I was
crying a little—I couldn't help it. "Lefty was like
one of my pets. I wanted to keep him with me forever."

"I know. But sometimes you have to let go of
someone you love because that's what's best for
them."

I thought about my futile visit with Jack the
Sunday before. "Maybe," I said, unconvinced.

We got to work. I tried to focus, but it was useless.
I was supposed to be helping him splint the wing of
an osprey with a minor injury, but every time he
asked me to hand him some supplies or instruments,
I gave him the wrong thing. "You're really distracted,
Laurel," Carlos said. "Thinking about Lefty?"

"Actually, I'm thinking about Jack." Flipping
my hair aside, I looked at Carlos. "Remember
him? The guy I was going out with."

"Yeah, I remember," said Carlos.

The bird's wing was finished. I followed Carlos
as he carried the osprey back to its cage. "Well, it's

been almost a month since we broke up, and he's as mad at me as ever. I'm *not* sorry we broke up," I added so Carlos wouldn't get the wrong impression. I wanted him to know I was unattached, just in case. "But I'm afraid we'll never be friends again. Why can't we go back to the way we were before we started dating? It doesn't make sense!"

Carlos laughed as he turned away from the cage. "Who said relationships made sense? Take me and Emily."

Emily? I thought. His sister? His cat? His hairstylist? "Emily?" I asked.

"My girlfriend."

"Oh." I felt myself blush, and I prayed Carlos would never, ever guess that for a minute there I'd actually imagined he could be a little bit interested in me. Of course he has a girlfriend, I thought. You idiot, Laurel.

Carlos handed me a tub of bird feed. We moved along the row of cages, filling seed trays. "We keep playing these dumb games. Like, she was mad because I didn't go to Florida for spring break with her. I just didn't have the cash. And now I'm trying to figure out a way for us to be together over summer vacation and she acts like she couldn't care less about that."

"She probably wants to be with you," I commented, imagining how I'd feel in Emily's place. "Maybe she's worried that you'll take her for granted or something."

"That's my point," Carlos said. "Who knows,

right? She has her own private heart. And I have mine and you have yours and Jack has his."

"You and Emily are working things out, though, right?"

"We broke up for a while last fall and then got back together," Carlos answered. "I guess my advice about Jack is just to let things take their course. What's meant to be will be."

At the end of the day Carlos sat down at the desk in the office to type up some notes while I went outside to play with a pair of orphaned coyote pups. The trees were getting really leafy, and it was fun to watch the pups pounce on the shifting patterns of sun and shade on the ground.

I sat on the grass, leaning back on my hands, and looked up into the sky. Suddenly I started to laugh. Carlos and me as a couple, I thought. Yeah, right! Straightening up, I wrapped my arms around my knees and glanced toward the parking lot. Carlos was climbing into his car—he waved in my direction. Who knows, though? I mused. What had he said? What will be, will be? Maybe someday . . .

I put the coyotes back in their pen and brushed the grass and dirt off the legs of my overalls. I'd walked to work that morning, and I headed home by way of the beach.

In the late afternoon light the ocean was brilliantly blue. A couple of sailboats zigzagged along the horizon. The beach, deserted and seaweed strewn in winter, was dotted with people. Summer was just around the corner.

I stopped to watch a little girl playing catch with her father. They were both wearing Boston Red Sox caps, and all at once I felt a stab of grief so intense, I had to sit down on a rock.

I remembered Dad teaching Daisy how to throw. I could picture us all, as vividly as if it had been yesterday. We were all outside in the grassy yard of the big house one summer evening. Dad tossed grounders for Daisy; she scooped them up in her glove with ease. Rose had been helping Mom in the garden. Lily was playing with her dolls while I collected fireflies in a mason jar.

I turned my head to look out at the ocean. The water was calm. Hard to believe on a day like this that the sea could turn into a monster that devoured fishermen and their boats.

Closing my eyes, I took a deep breath of sea air. It filled my lungs with salty, cool freshness. "I miss you, Dad," I whispered. "I miss you, Daze."

With a sigh, I stood up. The little girl and her father had gone home.

Walking along the shore, I stopped every few yards to study a tide pool or pick up a clamshell. Gulls screeched and sandpipers skittered along the edge of the surf, stabbing their pointy beaks into the wet sand in search of food. I stopped to take off my sneakers and socks and roll up my pants. Then, with my shoes in my hands, I walked a few steps into the waves.

The Atlantic felt like ice. I sucked in my breath as my toes went instantly numb. I stayed in the water, though, waiting for it to happen. And it did. As the wild peace of the sea filled me, I felt something deep in my bones. I knew I'd always miss my father and my sister, but I would make it without them. I'd make it without Jack, too, if I had to, and I wasn't even really that disappointed that Carlos had a girlfriend. Maybe I didn't march to the same drummer as most people, but I could do things on my own and do them well. That was what I'd learned, little by little, in the year I turned sixteen. I was complete by myself.

Which wasn't to say I didn't need people. When my feet were dry, I put my shoes back on and hurried toward town. Mom had taken the weekend off to spend time with me and Lily—she was probably already cooking dinner. Lily would be writing a story, and Snickers would be waiting for her walk.

I couldn't wait to get home.

Fourteen

The rest of May passed in a whirl. The weekend before the wedding Mom, Lily, Hal, and I went down to Boston for Rose's and Stephen's commencements. We were so proud of Rose in her black gown and mortarboard, and when her a cappella group sang at a big postgraduation party, I was pretty sure I had the prettiest, coolest, most talented sister in the world.

The first Friday in June, back in Maine, Stephen's parents hosted a rehearsal dinner at the Harborside. Later on at home, even though it was after ten, we were all still running around. "I'll never be able to sleep," Rose said as she checked over her to-do list. "I'm getting married tomorrow!"

Mom was steaming shrimp. "Here's a project for you, then," she told Rose. "Check in with Sue Smith about the flowers."

Mrs. Smith, an old Lighthouse Road neighbor and Mom's good friend, was doing the bouquets and centerpieces. While Rose got on the phone to call her, Lily and I went upstairs. "Let's wrap our present," she suggested.

We'd pooled our savings to buy a gift for Rose and Stephen: an engraved picture frame for them to put their wedding photo in. Lily took the box out of her closet, along with a roll of pink-and-white wrapping paper. "I think they're really going to like it," she predicted.

I looked at the frame one more time while Lily cut the paper. "I think so, too."

Lily put the lid back on the box and started to wrap it. Then she stopped and gazed at me with sad eyes. For a moment we were pensive and still. Would anything ever feel right without Daisy?

"I still miss her all the time," Lily said.

I nodded. "Me too."

Lily sighed and then got back to work. She taped the package briskly while I took a roll of ribbon and made curls with the scissors blade. "How many people do you suppose will come to the wedding tomorrow?" she asked.

"Rose said about seventy."

"Hmmm." Lily gave me a sly look. "I wonder if there will be any *surprise* guests?"

I raised my eyebrows. "You mean, gate-crashers?"

Lily giggled. "No. Well, I guess we'll see, won't we?"

"I guess so," I said, even though I had no idea what she was talking about.

We tied the ribbon onto the package and then took turns writing in the card. When Lily handed me the pen, I read what she'd written: *To the most wonderful big sister in the world and the sweetest brother-in-law I could ever hope for. Wishing you a life-time of happiness together. Love, Lily.*

I hesitated. Lily had said it all; what could I add? Then I thought of something. For once I found the words to fit what I was feeling. "Thanks for always being there, you two," I scribbled. "I love you both so much. And Rose, let's be best friends as well as sisters forever."

The first Saturday in June dawned sunny and clear. "Hallelujah," Rose exclaimed at breakfast. "It was so muggy last night, I was sure it would be pouring today. But look at that glorious blue sky!"

None of us could eat much. We were all too excited. After breakfast Rose went for a jog to calm her nerves. Then she was in the shower for about an hour. Then it was time to get ready.

I let Rose have my room and I changed in Lily's. Lily and I were putting on our shoes when Rose called out to us, "Hey, guys. I need your help."

Lily and I crossed the hall. Rose was standing in the middle of my room, half in the wedding dress. "Will someone zip me?" she asked.

I zipped Rose up. She fidgeted with the sleeves of the wedding dress, pushing them off her shoulders a little bit. "Time for the hair," she announced.

Rose had decided to wear her hair in a loose French twist. Lily helped her pin it up, and then she positioned the hair comb from which the long veil fluttered. "'Something old, something new, something borrowed, something blue,'" Lily recited.

"Thanks for reminding me," Rose said. She handed me a strand of pearls. "These are Mom's. Something borrowed."

"What about something blue?" I asked as I hooked the pearls around Rose's neck.

She grinned. "My underpants."

"The dress is old," Lily said.

"And the veil is new," Rose said. She patted the necklace. "There. I'm ready."

Lily and I stood on either side of Rose in front of the mirror. We looked at our reflection. Rose smiled. "What do you think?"

I stared. I couldn't believe this was my sister, the girl I'd grown up with, the girl with long hair and bare feet who was always singing. Because she wasn't a girl anymore; the long white dress had transformed her into a woman.

I thought about how we all still missed Daisy more than we could bear sometimes. There should have been four sisters gazing together into the mirror and into the future. But the more we worked at it, the better we were getting at being just three. I felt closer to Rose and Lily all the time.

"You look beautiful, Rose," I said, my eyes damp.

Lily was misty, too. "Oh, Rose."

Lily and I leaned close to Rose, and we had a group hug. "Don't make me cry," Rose grumbled.

"My mascara will run!" But she held us tightly for a minute, as if knowing that when she let go, she would step away from us into another identity, another life.

"Look at you."

The three of us turned to see Mom standing in the doorway. She was beautiful, too, in a cornflower blue chiffon dress. "Oh, Rose," she said, echoing Lily. "I can't believe it. My oldest girl is a bride."

Smiling through their tears, Rose and Mom embraced for a long moment. "The limo's here to take you to the church," Mom told Rose. "Are you ready?"

Rose looked at me and Lily. We stepped to her side, and she took our hands, giving them a squeeze. "I'm ready," she said.

Peeking through the door to the chapel with Lily while Val and Elizabeth helped Rose adjust her veil, I could see that the little church was full. The organist, Mrs. Enright, was playing an introit. Flanked by his groomsmen, Stephen stood at the altar with Reverend Beecher, his hands clasped in front of him and a nervous, expectant smile on his face. "One more minute," I whispered to Rose. "Everyone's here!"

We lined up in the hall: Lily first because she was the shortest, then Valerie and Elizabeth, and finally me, the maid of honor. Rose was last. Mom and Hal had offered to walk with her, but she'd decided to walk down the aisle by herself. "Daddy will be with me in spirit," she'd said. "I won't be alone."

Now Mrs. Enright started playing the Handel piece Rose and Stephen had chosen for the processional. "This is it!" Val whispered.

Clutching her bouquet, Lily looked over her shoulder at me. I nodded. "Go ahead."

One by one, the bridesmaids proceeded down the aisle. I knew Lily was nervous, but it didn't show—she looked elegant and calm. When my turn came, I waited an extra beat. Standing behind me, Rose touched my arm. She knew why I'd waited. It was Daisy's turn. Daisy was here in spirit, too.

I began walking down the aisle, wishing I had Lily's grace and poise. I almost didn't make it to the altar because I spotted Mr. and Mrs. Harrison sitting in the third row on the left side . . . and Jack was with them. When his eyes met mine, I was so startled, I tripped a little. Just what I'd been most afraid would happen! Luckily I managed to recover enough to avoid falling flat on my face, and I made it to the altar in one piece, although I was beet red from the neck up.

At the front of the church, the bridesmaids lined up opposite the groomsmen and everyone turned to face the door. When Rose appeared, a vision in her long white gown with the bouquet of pink rosebuds held before her, a collective sigh filled the church. I saw Gram start crying and Hal hand Mom a handkerchief. The most wonderful thing of all, though, was Stephen's face. He'd known Rose since she was sixteen, but at that moment it was as if he were seeing her for the first time and he couldn't believe his good fortune. Joy, amazement, and gratitude radiated from his eyes. And love. Most of all, love.

Rose reached the altar. Stephen held out his hand to her and she stepped to his side, her gaze never leaving his. "Dearly beloved," the minister began.

We all cried during the ceremony because weddings are emotional and because it was impossible not to remember the last time all our friends and relatives had gathered together in this church—for Daisy's funeral. By the time we arrived at the Mathiases' house for the reception, though, the mood had lightened.

"We're married!" Rose squealed, throwing her arms around Stephen even though they were supposed to be posing for a formal portrait. "Yippee!"

Stephen's parents' sprawling backyard was bordered by formal gardens—the perfect setting for a wedding. There were buffet tables set up under a white-canopied tent, and Mom's catering assistant, Sarah, was circulating among the guests, passing out glasses of champagne. I saw Jack standing with Lily. I knew I should go talk to him. I still couldn't believe he'd come.

Feeling shy, I made my way over. "Hi, Jack," I

said. Before I could stop her, Lily melted away into the crowd, leaving us alone.

"Hi," Jack said.

We stood there, holding our glasses of sparkling punch. "Wasn't it a nice ceremony?" I asked after a long pause.

"Rose is a beautiful bride," Jack replied.

"So. I didn't expect you to be here. I'm glad," I added softly.

Jack nodded in the direction Lily had gone. "You can thank your little sister."

"Lily?" I wrinkled my eyebrows. "What do you mean?"

"She came over a couple of days ago," Jack explained, "and practically begged me to come to the wedding. She said I had to, or you'd be too upset to properly carry out your maid of honor duties."

So that was why she was so mysterious, hinting about surprise wedding guests! I thought. The corners of Jack's lips twitched a little. Was he actually going to smile? "What a meddler." I shook my head.

"She meant well."

Just then I spotted Lily watching us from a distance. When she caught my eye, she blew me a kiss. "It's true. She did," I agreed. Silence fell over us again. "Well," I said.

"Well."

"Thanks. I *am* glad you came."

He turned his head away. "Um." He cleared his throat. "I think I'll go get some food."

"And I should talk to my grandparents. See you later?"

"Yep."

Jack strode off toward the tent. That wasn't so bad, I thought, wistful for the days when Jack and I could talk for hours. A little stiff, but it could've been worse.

Lily appeared at my elbow. "Well?"

"You're a busybody, you know that?"

"Are you going to be friends again or not?"

I looked after Jack. Weddings make you feel good about the future, and a tiny flower of hope blossomed in my heart. "I think we might," I answered.

Mom and Sarah and our other friends who'd helped cook did a great job—the food was delicious. When everyone had eaten, it was time for Rose and Stephen to cut the cake, which was devil's food with white butter cream icing and a garnish of pink sugar rosebuds.

More champagne was poured, and it was time for toasts. Mr. Mathias went first. "On behalf of Anne and myself, thank you, Maggie and Hal, for putting together this splendid party," he said, lifting his glass. "We already thought of Rose as our daughter, and we're delighted to welcome her officially into our family."

Hal said a few words, and so did Stephen's best man, his college roommate, George. Then Stephen himself stepped forward. "In case anyone here doesn't already know it," he began, slipping his arm around Rose's waist, "I am the luckiest man alive."

"Here, here!" everyone cried.

"My best friend, Rose Annabelle Walker, is now my wife. I can't imagine greater happiness."

Stephen and Rose kissed. Everybody clapped.

"I had an ulterior motive in marrying Rose, though," Stephen went on, a twinkle in his eye. "This way I get to be part of her family forever, and as you've all experienced today, her mom, Maggie, is the world's best cook. I plan to enjoy many, many meals at her table in the years to come."

Stephen winked at Mom. There was more laughter. "And as if the two I had weren't enough, I also get two new sisters," Stephen said. "I think Lily and Laurel both know how special they are to me. And today I know we're all remembering Rose's sister Daisy and how much she meant to us. Her memory will always be Rose's and my most precious possession."

For a moment we were all silent. I felt a hand on my shoulder. Turning, I saw that Jack had stepped up behind me. Lifting my hand, I placed it over his.

"Finally, I'd like to thank you all for being here to witness our vows," Stephen concluded. He smiled down at his bride. "There's no backing out now. You're stuck with me, Rose!"

Stephen and Rose kissed again. There was

more clapping and laughing, and then the band started playing Rose's favorite Beatles song, "If I Fell." Stephen led Rose to the dance floor that was set up at one end of the tent and took her gently in his arms.

Alone, Stephen and Rose circled the floor. Jack had taken his hand from my shoulder and moved a few steps away. Lily was standing next to me now. "Their first dance as husband and wife," she said with a sentimental sniffle.

Watching Rose and Stephen, I got sniffly, too. "They're so perfect together," I said.

Lily nodded. "Someday you'll get married to the perfect person, too."

That day seemed a long, long way off . . . which was fine with me. When the first song ended, other couples crowded onto the dance floor. Jack came back over. "Would you like to dance, Laurel?" he asked formally.

We danced one song, holding each other at arm's length. Still, the fact that he asked me at all was a gesture I appreciated. Then Jack asked Lily to dance, and I moved onto the grass to watch.

I want to save this moment, I thought, trying to memorize every detail of the scene. Rose in Mom's wedding gown with her bridal veil whirling out behind her as she and Stephen spun on the dance floor; Lily and Jack dancing awkwardly and laughing; Mom and Hal lifting their champagne glasses in a private toast; the lush, romantic scent of roses in the air; overhead, the sun bright in the flawless

June sky; and in the distance the deep, timeless blue of the sea.

My expression grew pensive as I thought about the great adventure my older sister and her husband were embarking upon. My future will be an adventure, too, I reflected. School was almost over, and another long summer stretched out ahead of me. I'd be working full-time at the Wildlife Rescue Center, and since I'd already taken all the science classes offered at South Regional, I also planned to register for a course at the community college—I'd get a jump on my college credits.

Then it will be fall again, I thought. My senior year in high school. I'll turn seventeen. An ache entered my heart. Along with my birthday would come another anniversary . . . one year since Daisy's death.

"What are you thinking about, Toad?"

I blinked. I hadn't even noticed that the music had stopped and my sister, the bride, had come over to me. "I was thinking about Daisy," I admitted.

Rose put her arms around me. "I miss her today, don't you?"

I nodded. "But I hate being sad on your wedding day."

We stepped apart again. "It's okay," she said. "I'm a little sad, too, underneath the happiness. Daisy wouldn't want us to mope, though. She'd say, 'Get out there, girls, and *party!*'"

I knew Rose was right. Our family had experienced more than our share of tragedy, but we also seemed to have more than our share of love.

I smiled at Rose. "Then let's party."

Rose hooked her arm through mine, and together we walked back to the celebration.

My three older sisters have always known who they were. Rose has her music. Daisy was a born athlete. Laurel loves animals.

I always thought that by the year I turned sixteen, I would have discovered something that made me special, too. But what do I have? Weird clothes? Bad handwriting? Somehow, these things don't seem to measure up.

But lately I've discovered how to make people— even the guy of my dreams—pay attention to me. All I have to do is pretend to be someone I'm not . . . .

**Will Lily's dreams come true . . .
or backfire?**

**Find out in
The Year I Turned Sixteen #4:
*Lily***

THE YEAR

I TURNED

Sixteen

Four sisters. Four stories.